# POSTCARD PIMLICO

by
Paul Barrell

In memory of John Armstrong 1961–2010

To the late Paul Hessian, who should have written a book

To the late Arthur Hopcraft, who never knew I could write

# JOHN'S DEAD
## March 24th 2010

He didn't know why but today he felt different: maybe it was the music, maybe it was the promise of spring that lifted his flagging spirits.

Squeezing his Range Rover through the narrow back streets of Battersea, John's deep baritone voice rose steadily as he sang along to his playlist. He thought about his son, how fast he was growing and looked forward to the day when his wife would allow Harrison to join him at training. He held the thought for a few seconds as he reversed into a parking space next to the common. The early arrivals were already throwing the ball around and he leant over and grabbed his bag from the back seat. In a side pocket was the last batch of invitations to his fiftieth birthday celebration.

One minute he was running with the ball, swerving and feinting, avoiding the outstretched hands of the opposition, the next his heart inexplicably stopped pumping blood to his vital organs. As the players shadows lengthened and the red sun sank behind rows of silver birch his six foot two frame collapsed into the freshly mown spring grass.

Everyone presumed he would get up, dust himself down and return to the fray as he always did. This time he didn't. The players stopped and turned, their sweaty faces etched with concern. Another few seconds passed and fear replaced concern as they huddled over his lifeless body. Over by the kit bags and water bottles a small crowd of onlookers raised the alarm on their mobile phones.

John never saw it coming. He was dead before he hit the ground. It was a momentous tragedy. He was highly respected, the dynamic force behind a top Advertising Agency. His vision had taken the company to new heights and along the way he had acquired the trappings of London's new money. He left in his wake a listed company, a beautiful Swiss wife and two young children, but very few knew anything about his personal life. A few close friends speculated about his life before, if speculated was the right word to use about a man who never spoke about his past.

That evening a twin's bond was extinguished and John's untimely death was to have much wider ramifications for us all.

# THE REUNION
## March 31st 2010

It began with a phone call.

I looked at the display on my phone. The caller I.D. was unknown. Not many people had my mobile number and I deliberated about taking the call.

*What the hell.*

I held my breath and answered.

'John's dead.'

No hello, just straight to the point. Two totally numbing words...then, an unsettling silence!

The voice was familiar but it took a few more seconds for me to be sure.

*When? How?*

'Fuck, is that really you?'

There were a million questions I wanted to ask, but not now. The caller's voice was distinctive, rounded vowels with the cadence of privilege. Public School gravitas.

'He died a week ago. A heart attack.'

A long silence followed and it took a while for the bombshell to sink in.

'The funeral is in two weeks, I'll send you details of how to get to the church. It's down South, not far from where my parents used to live.'

I remembered Sunday lunch with Mr and Mrs Armstrong. The decanted wine, the finest silver, the polite stilted conversation. I remembered it all.

'…and I've just spoken to Monty'.

'Monty!' I exclaimed. Surprise replaced the earlier consternation in my voice.

'Can you make it then? I want you to be there mate. It's been too long.'

*Mate.*

Was I still his mate? For a few seconds I chewed over the connotations of the word 'mate'. My hand shook as I mentally added it up, twenty five years and counting since I'd seen them.

'That's the understatement of the century,' I replied. But Charles ignored the sarcasm.

'Listen we need to meet up.' He said it all very matter-of-factly. It was like he was reading from a script, or we had only spoken yesterday.

I took a deep breath and exhaled very slowly. The phone call was like a bolt of electricity, lighting up long forgotten corridors to the past. To be honest, I was in shock, paralysed by the whole surreal conversation. Surely it was a sick joke. No, surely Charles wouldn't joke about something as serious as this, or would he? But with Charles you never knew.

I cleared my throat and the rollercoaster began.

'Are you still there?' There was an urgency to his voice.

I stood looking at the small phone in my hand. Sharp memories came flooding back. I choked back an overwhelming urge to cry, but then I always had been riddled with insecurities, a slave to my emotions.

'Ben! Talk to me.'

*John dead.*

I hadn't known him that well, a few nights out, a few weeks holiday together but I couldn't say I really knew him. Not like Charles and Monty. I gripped the phone and tried not to let Charles hear the tremor in my voice. In the end curiosity got the better of me.

'Of course, where shall we meet?'

## April 4th 2010

A week and a half later, I waited for two men I hadn't seen since the eighties. Two men I spent the best three years of my life with, two men I trusted unconditionally. We drank together, slept together, cried together and laughed together. We covered each other's back, and swore by the code. In a strange, non-gay way I loved them like the brothers I hadn't had.

I ordered a drink from the barman. I tried not to think about my own mortality but I couldn't help it. I wondered who would be at the funeral. I imagined a gaudy affair like that of Paula Yates; a gathering of eighties survivors, a final hurrah. Men in Ray Bans, dark Issy Miyake suits, women in stilettos, tailored-coats, wrap-arounds pushed up into big hair. I'd had time to think about things more clearly since the phone call, and like the rising bubbles in my glass of prosecco, beneath the surface a sense of unease grew.

*Why now?*

A tragedy like this united people, I'd seen it happen countless times over the years. But was it really that simple? And what of Monty? Was he still under Charles' spell? I reached for an olive and chewed thoughtfully round the stone, but the more I thought about it the more uncomfortable I began to feel.

I slouched in a corner booth and watched the Cheshire set come and go. The plush leather furniture and muted lighting exuded a warm reddish glow that should have calmed and soothed. I wanted to feel relaxed but I wasn't and my mind began to wander. I thought of my sister. They both knew her; they knew her about as well as I knew John. Would I be tracking them down, making the same calls if she had died? But then this wasn't the same, how could it be, this was Charles.

My mobile vibrated on the marble table, making me jump. I was nervous as hell, I just couldn't understand why. My phone glowed. Blue sonar blips, as a text came through.

*Running late.*

I expelled air through my nose, grinding my back teeth, a nervous habit that had worsened over the years. Still the same Charles. Always brusque, always economical with his words.

*Was I still scared of him?*

I imagined him sitting in front of me, picking his teeth with a folded piece of card, doing that thing he did with his eyebrow. Searching for weakness. Trying to control me.

I inspected my own fleshy visage in the mirrored wall beside me. I wished I looked better but I looked gaunt and washed out. I pulled on the skin around my eyes, making the age lines momentarily disappear, a little Botox wouldn't go amiss I thought. Would Charles look the same? I shivered, but it wasn't caused by the air conditioning. Someone walked over my grave.

*Over twenty five years.*

It was a long time in anyone's book. A few years back I'd searched Facebook and Twitter for Monty but drew a blank. Charles had a dormant Twitter account and his Facebook page gave little clues as to his whereabouts. If I had understood DM I might have made an attempt at contact but I was stuck in the dark ages and my kids ridiculed me because I hadn't yet embraced the world of social networking.

I said a silent prayer. Please God, let Charles be less handsome, greyer, more craggy perhaps. I secretly hoped he looked like shit. He had been the archetypal Peter Pan but surely he couldn't work that magic now.

I tried to divert my thoughts. I gazed across the room at two women, perched like exotic birds on chrome stools, as they preened themselves in a smoked glass mirror. I reflected on another bar the three of us frequented, a subterranean cocktail bar on the King's Road. In 1982 it was our place, our hangout.

I stared absently at an abstract painting of three red poppies on the adjacent wall. The chitter chatter around me stilled, as if someone had flipped a dimmer switch and a Gershwin song began to play in my head. Time warped as my present and past intertwined. It was the oddest of feelings, my very own time machine.

# BEN'S STORY
## July 1984

*It had all started and ended here.*

*Laughter and music drifted up narrow wooden stairs. A familiar refrain beckoned me down to a shabby, smoky room drenched in the sweet tang of exotic liqueurs, cannabis and something cathedral-like, incense or myrrh.*

*I stepped over the sagging bottom step and from the retro jukebox under the stairs, came the telltale Celtic fiddle and rasping drum beat of Dexys Midnight Runners.*

*Across the room lit by a solitary wax laden candle, two girls with back-combed hair and thick black eyeliner sat at a heavily pock-marked wooden table. Wine glasses full to the brim as they shared a hushed, intimate conversation. The filters of their cigarettes were smeared with bright red lipstick and smoke drifted upwards in mystical spirals from a silver foil ashtray.*

*I leaned against a pillar and watched the bar gradually fill. In the candlelight the girls could be mistaken for the female duo from a girl band. One girl, a red scarf tied in her hair, leant forward stripping the label from the nearly empty bottle of cheap Italian wine. I rolled my Zippo across a denim clad leg, lit a cigarette and exhaled perfectly formed smoke rings that hung in the air like the opening credits from 'Captain Scarlet and the Mysterons.' It was a skill I practised with fervour. That night I felt like the villainous Captain Black, watching in the shadows, all brooding looks and dark stubble. I raised the collar on my leather jacket and thrust a hand deep into my jeans pocket, my fingers searching for loose change. I moved confidently to the bar, ordered a drink and waited for my flatmates.*

*I moved closer to the girls. They were deep in conversation and just for a second I considered joining them, but I drew back at the last moment as I heard feet tap-tap-tapping on the stairs. I turned instinctively, running a list of acceptable excuses through my mind. My top ten plea bargains. An Arabic man and a young woman stumbled into the room, they obviously weren't regulars otherwise they would know about the worn bottom step. My stomach sank. It wasn't them.*

*Where the hell were they?*

*I shrugged my shoulders and cursed under my breath.*

I thought fleetingly about a recent female acquaintance and remembered that if I needed a bed for the night I didn't have far to travel. However, I hadn't given up completely on Charles and Monty.

The girl with the red scarf in her hair eyed me over her friend's shoulder. Blue eyes, long lashes. I was aware of her openly flirtatious demeanour as she mouthed something silently to her friend. She had no idea I was an accomplished lip-reader, courtesy of years spent with my partially deaf sister, a talent I had honed and used whenever a tricky situation needed decoding. Flattered but dismissive of their advances I stubbed out my cigarette on the wooden floor. I glanced at my watch. I had seen Holly Johnson wearing an identical one on TV and mine was an exact replica. It was 11.30. In the fuzzy haze of end of term euphoria had I missed something? I tried to convince myself that any second now they would appear on the stairs, laughing and joking; they always had.

A stool became vacant and I sat alone at the small corner bar, the deeply scored surface ingrained with graffiti and sticky with spilled spirits. I began to mull over stupid little details: in order to get our deposits *back we needed to return our flat keys to the agent. I had the telephone numbers for Charles' and Monty's parents in my address book, and for one crazy moment I considered phoning them to see if they knew anything.*

*I slapped my hand against my forehead. God, we were all supposed to be heading to Kent tomorrow to Steve's place. But then I realised I hadn't a clue where we were meeting or exactly where we were going. Steve's family were well-off, they owned a drinks company, and his brother had embraced the recent craze for wind surfing; more importantly, his parents were away for a whole month. However, fat lot of good that would do me because I didn't even know which village they lived in. Two weeks of partying lay ahead but we always relied on Charles to get us from A to B in his knackered Mini and he wasn't fucking here.*

*It had all happened so quickly, and I was totally unprepared. I considered my options. I wasn't sure who was left at number 64 and St George's Square was only a taxi ride away. Over the last few days everyone had been packing up to go their separate ways; perhaps Charles and Monty were saying their goodbyes. I tapped the bottom of my Marlboro packet and lit another cigarette as I weighed up whether it was worth the risk. In the end I decided to stay put and waited diligently until midnight, but still they didn't come.*

*Something was wrong.*

*Baz put 'High Society' into the tape deck. It was Monty's favourite music and I wondered if Louis Armstrong's gravelly voice and his signature trumpet blasts would lure Monty down from the street. But time had run out. Baz switched off the tape deck and began to restock the bar. He looked up and pointed to the clock on the wall; it was time to go.*

*The jukebox started up again one last time and reluctantly I climbed the wooden stairs. The rousing chorus of the song followed me up into the summer night air and my destiny beyond.*

\*

I was jolted back to the present, not by music but by raised voices, harsh northern accents. There was a commotion over to my left. Men in business suits jostled each other and a barman in braces and a tattoo on his neck attempted to diffuse the situation. The two women I had studied earlier looked irritated by the fracas and got up to leave. It appeared a drink had been accidentally spilt over someone; it was all a storm in a teacup.

I checked my watch again. I wondered if the bastards would come tonight. I wondered if they remembered like I did.

# AVONMORE ROAD
## December 1981

I was twenty when I left home and moved to London. The country was in the middle of the deepest recession since the 1920's and a winter of discontent loomed ominously on the horizon. The wave of euphoria around Margaret Thatcher's election victory had dwindled and she was dealing with widespread national unrest: around the coalpits of northern and middle England, disillusioned miners fought pitch battles with the police; Liverpudlians rioted, burning cars and their heritage; and within months the Argentinian army invaded the Falkland Islands. Our country soon teetered on the brink of war.

Under this mostly bleak backdrop, music became an integral soundtrack to student life. In the hub of a throbbing pre-AIDS metropolis New Romantics and New Wave jostled for dominance of the capitals airwaves. This was our time: a time for planning, self-indulgence, looking good and feeling immortal.

It turned out to be a harsh winter. One of the coldest for twenty years my mother said. Arctic conditions prevailed from December to March and most nights ice formed on the inside of the windows. There was no central heating so Charles taped up the windows with newspaper but it had little effect, Monty and I donned full thermals before ducking under the covers. It wasn't quite how the flat share had been portrayed to me when we sat in The Three Kings a few weeks before.

Set amongst crumbling guest houses our flat was on the first floor of a terraced, Victorian house near Olympia. Two weather-beaten colonnades stood either side of well-worn steps which led to a front door that needed a fresh coat of paint. The landlord invested neither time nor money on repairs and the front door was always ajar due to a broken lock; an open invitation to thieves and undesirables. The small balcony defied the laws of gravity, a potential death trap. I was sure one day it would plummet earthwards, causing the death of an unsuspecting visitor. Once you stepped inside it wasn't much better; the hallway was damp and musty, a solitary light bulb hung noose-like from the ceiling and wallpaper peeled from the walls. There was a wall-mounted payphone next to a cork message board, while directly ahead the uncarpeted stairs rose precipitously to the rest of the house.

The living room provided little warmth and the solitary gas fire leaked toxic, carbon monoxide into the air. Most nights we delayed bedtime, plying the gas meter with coins, until we were lulled to sleep by its deadly cocktail of emissions. In hindsight I think we were lucky not to suffer any long-term brain damage. The communal toilet never had any toilet paper and along with the latest editions of Tatler, Monty stacked up old Times newspapers for emergencies. Here hygiene levels never rose above those of a Third World country. The kitchen, if you could call it that, was no more than a cupboard with a two-ring cooker and a toaster. It was also on the landing and conveniently located next to the toilet.

If I needed to shower I had to visit the basement. It was a journey that took me past the door where two German lesbians lived, down into the sinister bowels of the building. The shower cubicle stood at the end of a gloomy corridor, a portal to another time, another place. It was lined with black plastic sheeting, not for the squeamish; it reminded me of a set from an S & M film and I tried to spend as little time down there as possible.

I only found out weeks later that my two new flat-mates were washing in much improved conditions in a bathroom on the second floor. They just hadn't bothered to tell me.

There was a small annex off the living room, with a green velvet curtain which served as a flimsy partition. Comically, the landlord heralded this as the second bedroom and Charles immediately commandeered this particular corner as his den. An overly ornate, fully stocked Georgian cocktail cabinet (courtesy of Monty's parents' antiques business) sat along one wall, juxtaposed with our only other furniture, three brightly-coloured deckchairs and a battered and bruised arm chair. Monty's friend worked at Athena and Grace Kelly took pride of place above the fire place, while Alpine vistas filled the gaps on the empty walls. It may have been a mere stepping stone before a move to a more prestigious postcode but it was my first taste of real freedom and I remembered those few months in W14 with great fondness.

During those bitterly long winter evenings we spent much of our free time at Baz and Annie's. Monty had stumbled upon the basement bar shortly after arriving in

London: a world of Blue Lagoons, Red Leb and amyl nitrate. It wasn't on any tourist map but its shabby, smoky atmosphere attracted a diverse audience from the Chelsea area: travellers, beatnicks, musicians and a hardcore of privileged kids who were searching for something different. Monty soon became part of the furniture and most nights he persuaded the owner to play music from 'High Society.' This soundtrack soon became not only ours but the bar's signature tune. You see Monty had old school class and his music interests belonged to a different era from the rest of us.

The owner was one of the early drink mixologists and every week Baz created a new cocktail for us, each one more potent than the last. His energetic partner Annie ran the small bistro upstairs and sent food down to us in a rickety dumb waiter that always got stuck. In a curious way I felt like the richest man alive, when we sat at the bar, side by side, putting the world to rights. I'm not sure why, but we decided to keep our den of iniquity a well-kept secret. As I said before, this was our place, our hangout.

Sometimes after three or four cocktails we would take a cab to another of our preferred haunts around Chelsea.

In The Australian or The Admiral Cod, we watched capricious, self-indulgent pop videos of our idols on the big screen. I was heavily into the buzzing music scene; every week there seemed to be another notable musical newcomer jostling for the top chart position and notoriety.

It was during these forays into the heart of SW1 that I started to understand the world Charles and Monty inhabited. The world of Public Schools, debutantes and old money. When they asked me to move in with them, I imagined a flat with a gold bell push, cigar boxes and crystal, but it was the antithesis. They chose to deny themselves items of personal luxury and instead concentrated on more hedonistic pursuits. Thinking back now I would describe them as aristocratic predators: they were far more interested in raucous evenings spent in bars and restaurants, and strangely put little value on their possessions, unless it was the latest hip flask from Fortnum's. In the beginning I was totally at odds with their wrecking ball 'modus operandi', although I can thank them for teaching me the complex art of tying a real bow tie. They described wild parties at the Hurlingham club, drunken days at Henley Regatta and expensive lunches at La Tante Claire. It was a steep learning curve coming from a bog standard middle class background and it took a while before I began to feel at ease in my new world. A world that soon became highly addictive.

While Charles and Monty were entrenched in the Sloane lifestyle, other Londoners including myself were heavily influenced by the flamboyant fashion of a new age. Almost overnight the capital's streets and bars became awash with a kaleidoscope of colours; girls in rah rah skirts, leg warmers and permed hair and boys in electric blue trousers, dress shirts and braided jackets. I began to adopt the androgynous look that new designers were promoting on billboards and in magazines. I felt comfortable in my new skin. I wanted to be different and quickly found a new identity.

We were from opposite ends of the social spectrum but we gelled and I soon became an integral part of a very special team. As the days and weeks passed my popularity and confidence grew, although if I dared overstep the mark Charles would bring me back to earth and remind me that I wasn't from 'good breeding' stock like they were. Sometimes money was tight or there was an overdue College assignment to complete and I spent my evening alone, in front of our small portable black and white television, or listening to my Sony Walkman. I was never neglected for long and if the weather permitted we cycled to a riverside pub for a few pints while we planned our evening's entertainment. Sometimes on rain sodden Sunday afternoons they took me to the Cinemac in Notting Hill Gate for my introduction to European culture. Unfortunately the new releases were often subtitled and I found them difficult to follow, but Monty assured me it was all part of my personal growth and as the dark clouds hovered menacingly over London I felt strangely immune to the anger and desperation felt by many.

By Monday we were ready to drag our frozen bodies back to the tube station again and run the gauntlet of the crowded, bone-shaking District line. Our daily commute ended at Victoria. It was here we attended Hotel School, budding Roux Brothers and Charles Forte's, our gastronomic and epicurean futures still to be decided. If indeed that was the direction in which we decided to travel.

# MONTY
## April 4th 2010

The wine bar filled quickly. I peered through the noisy throng and caught a glimpse of a thick-set man standing alone. I shuffled to the end of the banquette and was about to approach him when he turned his head. Sadly the Roman nose and facial features were not that of my old friend. I shrugged my shoulders and patted my jacket pocket, feeling for the photographs I had discovered after Charles' phone call.

Over the years I had often reconstructed a reunion in my mind where the three of us took a nostalgic journey, back to where it all started. I was genuinely looking forward to the evening but at the same time a knot of anxiety tightened in my chest. There was much about our past that puzzled me and I prayed this evening would be memorable for the right reasons. I didn't have to wait much longer to find out.

Monty arrived first, surveying the bar like a new batsman arriving at the crease. I laughed dryly at the spectacle; it was something he always did. Old habits die hard I thought. From a distance he looked the same, well, more or less. The unmistakable broad shoulders that had propped up hundreds of scrums; those same shoulders that protected us if things got out of hand; those same shoulders that carried us home when we were unable to put one foot in front of another. I felt my heart beat speed up. An electrical charge bristled the hairs on the nape my neck.

*Déja vu.*

I stood, raised my arm and beckoned him over. I felt anxious because I wasn't sure he would recognise me. He turned.

'Monty, over here,' I shouted above the music.

He looked unusually tanned and healthy. He was dressed in a V-neck cricket jumper, cords and brogues: standard Monty attire. I noticed his hairline had receded but it was still thick and curly, unlike mine. He approached the booth confidently and his round face broke into a grin. I inspected his features. Small crooked teeth, a cauliflower ear, while deep furrows creased his wide forehead. I stood up and moved towards him. I held out my arms and he gave me a bear hug just like the old days. It felt good, like your favourite food. For me it was like coming home.

He rested a large paw on my shoulder.

'Hello handsome.' Did I detect a slight 'Aussie' twang?

I felt tongue tied, bowled over by the occasion.

'So what have you been doing for the last twenty five years? Or is it longer?' He inspected me from top to toe but didn't comment on my changed appearance, which surprised me.

'God it's good to see you,' I stammered, any past misdemeanours temporarily forgotten.

Until he actually slid his broad frame into the semicircular booth his presence felt unreal, otherworldly, as if he had come back from the grave. I knew he was real but I wanted to touch him make sure his skin was warm, not ice cold.

He looked at my empty glass and I hurriedly ordered a bottle of white wine from a passing waitress. As the young girl meandered her way through the crowd I realised I hadn't asked Monty if he was happy with my choice. Wine was something we had never compromised on, even if we were strapped for cash, like I was tonight. I ran my finger down the list of white wines.

'Sancerre ok?'

'Spot on. I can't touch the vin rouge any more, my liver doesn't find it agreeable.' Monty squeezed my arm, and then my shoulder as if to demonstrate his frustration. I felt my slight frame buckle; he was still as strong as an ox.

'What about…?'

He let me go. 'Not any more buddy.'

I was surprised. I think he single-handedly kept the Quintas of Porto in business in the early eighties and his cheeks still had a ruddy complexion like tannin. I wondered what other surprises he had up his sleeve. He raised his glass to mine. Clink, clink, clink. Three times. Our code.

'Cheers! Here's to John…'

'And here's to us. Here's to still being here,' I replied.

'Here's to the "Pimlico Posse".'

A warm sensation engulfed me. I hadn't expected him to remember. I chastised myself in the same breath, of course he would remember. I savoured the wine for a second and then greedily gulped it down.

I looked around. 'Why can't he be on time? Did he text you?'

Charles was always late.

'He'll be late for his own...' Monty paused in mid-sentence. 'Merde. Il est toujours en retard,' he added.

During his time at Prep school Monty spent summer exchanges in Grenoble, his French was not fluent but he got by because he could mimic a rich Gauloise accent. Sadly his parents had grown apart, divorced and while his mother remained in the family home in Cheshire, his father started a new life further south. After Prep school he was dispatched to Wrekin College as a boarder, but he wasn't hugely academic and after Sixth Form he moved down to London. The streets were paved more with rubbish than gold but he was tenacious and suave and secured a front of house job at the Dorchester Hotel. His undying passion was rugby and during frequent coffee breaks in the refectory he kept us all entertained with tales of epic school tours. I never saw him play but he talked a good game and if England lost, which they did a fair bit back then, it ruined his entire week.

By his own admission Monty's early experiences with girls had been limited. The reason soon became obvious: He was unable to read the subtle signals of female desire. He never knew when to press pause on a story and sweep them off their feet to the bedroom. I don't think he was disinterested in sex, it just wasn't that high on his list of priorities. Monty preferred getting bladdered. If drinking had been an Olympic sport he would have won gold medal after gold medal.

His mother had been a model and socialite in the swinging sixties and it came as no surprise to Monty that she found a wealthy Jewish property magnate to marry second time around. It was a heady combination. I remember their first visit to our flat, when they arrived in an ostentatious yellow Rolls Royce, a vehicle so grand that upon their arrival net curtains twitched all the way along Avonmore Road.

She never gave Monty much notice of her intended visits and as her arrival grew closer we raced around like headless chickens vacuuming, dusting and preparing the Martinis. Gin was chilled, ice was emptied into a Moet ice bucket and bowls of olives and peanuts were placed strategically around the room.

We gathered up the detritus of our day to day living and stacked it all haphazardly in the back bedroom. If someone had foolishly opened the louvered doors to peek inside they would have been caught in an avalanche of debris.

After spending so much time preparing for the visit, we were dismayed Monty's mother and her new husband never stayed long. I think the deck chairs put them off, but she could have been more appreciative of our valiant efforts to entertain. Monty always made Martinis, even though he knew his mother would turn her nose up and opt instead for a gin and tonic, with a slice of lime. She never strayed far from the front door while we talked and after a brief resumé of her property portfolio, she placed a Coutts cheque on the mantelpiece and kissed Monty goodbye. Then they were out the door and back in the Roller. We always went out to eat as soon as they left and Monty always paid.

Monty held his glass to the light, swirled the straw coloured liquid around and lifted it to his nose. Then he sipped and rolled the wine around his mouth before he swallowed it with a delicate kiss of his lips. He looked at me his mouth curled up in appreciation. 'Excellent choice.'

He placed his glass back on the table. 'Fucking sad news, I thought it was an early April fool's joke. You know Charles.'

I recalled standing in my garden, the hills of the Peak

District in the distance. My wife was calling me from the kitchen but I didn't hear her. I just stared into space, lost in maelstrom of memories. Monty crossed himself. 'That's exactly how I felt when I took the call. It hasn't sunk in yet.'

I was fascinated by his religious foible. I was sure Monty was an atheist.

'Do you think Charles has had himself checked over?' I added

Monty sighed. 'I just hope he understands the implications.'

It seemed ominous that Charles' father had a fatal heart attack when we were in our third year and I deliberated over whether heart problems could be hereditary. I never coped well with bereavement and I couldn't shake John's face from my mind. I swallowed hard, restraining emotions that welled up deep inside of me.

'Only forty-nine. It could have been one of us. Charles said they were

planning a joint party, a big bash in Mayfair. It's an absolute tragedy.'

Monty nodded solemnly. 'Life's a bitch isn't it…By

the way I've forgotten when your birthday is?'

'November, Armistice day,' I answered.

Charles was six months older than me. If my memory served me right, Monty would have to wait until next year to reach his own half century.

'I haven't planned anything yet.'

Monty shook his head. 'Anyhow it doesn't seem important at the moment.'

I lowered my voice. 'I feel so sorry for his wife and kids.'

'Yes,' Monty nodded, 'She was Swiss, a gemologist, pretty too by all accounts. John met her at the Farm Club in Verbier. He had done really well for himself. The family lived in a big house in Battersea near Gordon Ramsay.'

'What did he do?'

'Gordon Ramsay? Come on Ben where have you been?'

'No, John.'

'While we were still pissing around he got a grown up job. He joined Unilever in his late twenties and rose swiftly up the corporate ladder.'

Monty fiddled with a gold signet ring on his left hand.

'Charles said he always knew the right people, he was a popular guy, never said a bad word about anyone. And he was a good looking bastard with it.'

In his own way Charles was handsome and he hated the fact that people thought John was better looking. The two boys were born within minutes of each other but entirely different when it came to their genetic make-up.

'John ended up in advertising. Lots of travelling, parties and stress. Apparently he was on medication to help him sleep.'

'Maybe it was the drugs?'

'I don't know. Charles wasn't forthcoming with the gory details.'

'I've thought about him often since I heard the news. When we all lived in London didn't he work for a while as a chauffeur for some high end Limo company?'

Monty looked away, momentarily distracted. 'Let's say he led a colourful life.'

Maybe I imagined it but I felt something slip behind the mask. A fleeting sense of disquiet filled the space between us. No sooner had it appeared it was gone.

Monty sighed. 'He had everything he wanted. It's such a waste. There will be a big turnout for him. We could go down together if you want? I'm staying up here for a while, mum needs some help with one of her properties.'

The funeral played on my mind, I felt like an outsider now and I considered making a polite excuse. After all, it was a long way to go for a few hours and I wouldn't know anyone apart from my old flat mates. After all, we had scattered ourselves to the four corners of the UK and I would hardly be missed if I opted not to attend. Monty waited patiently for me to reply. I tried not to sound indecisive, yet that's exactly how I felt.

'Yeah, why not,' I said eventually.

Monty slapped me between my shoulders blades. 'Good lad.'

It was evident Monty knew much more about John's life than I did and I presumed he must have had some contact with the family over the years. I wanted to grab his arm and scream: why did you both hide away?

*What the fuck have you and Charles been up to?*

But I didn't. I reined in my frustration, biding my time. I swirled the wine in my own glass, trying hard to forget my future. 'So tell me, I heard you were setting up hotels in Cambodia and Vietnam.'

'You're a little behind the times, I've been back for a few years now. I may go back if the right offer comes in.'

'Vietnam's on my bucket list.' Ever since I could remember I'd been fascinated by its heritage and more recently its conflicts.

'You must go, trust me, the food and culture are mind-blowing.'

I nodded, not sure how I was ever going to hit the high-life again.

'Anyway, you look really well. Does your mother still have her place in the States?'

'You've got a good memory.'

Monty checked over his shoulder, lifted his shirt, grinned and showed me his tanned, hirsute chest.

'Jealous?'

I cracked a half-smile. 'A little.' I was of course. I used to be the one who kept my tan the longest.

'Mum still spends the winter there. I get to go a couple of times a year if I want to. I've actually just got back from Nevada. Do you remember my step-brother?'

I held my hand three feet from the floor. 'Sebastian, that little shrimp.'

'He is no longer a little shrimp, more Nordic Adonis. He got the Swedish looks, lucky bastard.'

Anita, Monty's step mum was from Stockholm.

'His film career has just taken off, from humble beginnings as an apprentice cameraman to the lofty heights of a fully-fledged director.'

I slapped my thigh. 'Good for him. It's funny to imagine him all grown up, he was always your baby brother.'

Monty smiled fondly at the memory.

'He rang me out of the blue while I was kicking my heels back in the UK.'

A bit like Charles I thought.

'I owed him a favour. A debt from way back.'

I wondered what sort of debt Monty had rung up with his step brother, I wanted to pry but decided it wasn't any of my business.

'What sort of film was he shooting?'

Monty put his glass down. 'Don't laugh, but Sebastian's illustrious career started in low-budget porn, this was not exactly a step up, more a shift sideways. It was an homage to the great Pharaohs. The crew built this really tacky section of Pyramid out of foam blocks, you would have laughed if you'd seen it.'

'Why not make it in Egypt, they have real pyramids there.'

Monty laughed. 'I think it was safer to shoot in the States and the grub's better.'

'So, was it all brooding Mark Antonys and maidens bathing in goats' milk?'

Monty paused. 'Not exactly. The film had an interesting story line though.'

He leant in close and whispered something in my ear.

I nearly choked on my wine. 'Jesus Christ! Zombies!' I spluttered, recalling the three of us, drunk as skunks watching 'Dawn of the Dead.'

'They bussed in dozens of extras. I was there for four weeks with a bunch of beer swilling rednecks but Seb made sure I was looked after.'

Monty flicked his fingers in the way rappers indicated they'd got a result.

'All expenses paid.'

It seemed at odds with his once stuffy image, but I reflected that maybe over the years he had begun to embrace more popular culture?

I dabbed at the wet mark on my shirt with a napkin, I

was still obsessive when it came to my appearance.

'It doesn't sound like he'll be up for an Oscar! So what was this work of cinematic brilliance called?'

'To be honest it was a shit film, I can't even remember its title now. You've seen one B grade gore fest you've seen them all.'

My upbeat tone belied the fact I was feeling empty inside. 'Oh well it sounds like you had a blast in, where did you say, Nevada?'

Monty gave me a knowing look followed by a cheeky grin.

'What about you, any weird shit happen to you over the years?'

I thought about my short list of ups and my long list of downs, especially my run in with HM Customs.

'No not really,' I replied absently.

'You said earlier you moved up here to escape. Escape from what?'

I wasn't sure myself, and for a moment I struggled for something to say. I wanted to tell him I was sorting my shit out. I contemplated telling him about the intended book, but I hesitated.

'If you want to know the truth, I got fed up with

chasing the elusive pot of gold.'

Monty nodded. 'That's London for you.'

'It's so much more peaceful up here, I needed to do something different. '

'Anyway you're happy up here by all accounts, that's all that matters. I heard you married and have kids.'

Monty didn't wait for me to reply. I sensed it wasn't a direction he really wanted the conversation to head in.

I tried to prevent envy washing over me, but it was difficult. I imagined an entire month away and I think Monty sensed my disposition change. He had always inclined towards diplomacy rather than confrontation.

'Look this whole film experience wasn't that glamorous really. I was only an extra and I spent most of my time collecting up severed limbs, trying to match them to the right body.'

I laughed half-heartedly as I reflected that these madcap shenanigans never happened to me anymore. My life had become boring and routine. I sipped my Sancerre thoughtfully; crisp, citrus flavours. The wine fizzed on my tongue like a starburst of memories and I recalled one of Monty's more impressive tales. It occurred on the Greek island of Ios. In a bar overlooking the quaint port,

Monty traded Tequila slammers with the Island's returning champion. They drank shots long into the night but just as victory was within Monty's grasp he collapsed, alive but unconscious. The local villager received the victory plaudits and humbly admitted he had never known anyone drink like Monty had that evening. The new champion went home to sleep it off and never woke up! The following day Monty returned to the bar and became the new champion by default. He was hailed by the locals as some sort of God and offered free Tequila for the rest of his holiday.

'Hercules,' they shouted in Greek as they paraded him round the small taverna on their shoulders. Someone took his photo and put it behind the bar; who knows it may still be there today. Monty the legend was born. I looked at the colossus sitting next me and I wondered how often he had recited it over the intervening years. Maybe we would hear it again tonight.

Monty scratched his head and pulled at his blonde curls. He was watching me, at least I thought he was watching me. Could he tell what I was thinking? Then he closed his eyes as if in deep contemplation. It was a little disconcerting but after a few seconds he opened them and returned to his film experiences in Nevada.

'I have to admit it was a tad surreal, especially when we had a break in filming. I supervised the catering from a chrome trailer and had to keep order in the ranks, as lines of limbless Egyptians queued for a quarter-pounder and fries. Once the blazing sun came up it was like someone had opened the door to a furnace. Look at me, I think I lost a stone!'

He did indeed look healthy and I patted his stomach affectionately. 'You look trim.'

'Thanks. I was exhausted at the end of each day and I literally crawled back to my trailer. It was decent enough but the antiquated air con made a racket like a spin dryer and kept me awake most of the night, when all I wanted to do was sleep like a baby.'

Unlike Charles who always interrupted, I listened diligently, drinking in the fable. Frankly I didn't need to hear my own voice all the time and had always been a good listener. Monty's monologues had always been worth hearing. He had that rare ability which drew the listener in; it didn't matter whether you believed him or not, he ensnared you.

Monty paused again and rubbed his temples. For a

moment I felt unsettled.

'Sorry Ben, I keep getting these damn headaches. Can you get me a glass of water so I can take one of these?'

Monty produced a tin and tapped out a small white pill into his palm.

I couldn't hide my concern.

'Of course, don't go anywhere I'll be right back.' The moment I said it, I regretted the connotation. But Monty didn't seem to notice the foot-in-mouth slip.

The bar was two deep so I went to the far end where a young guy was washing glasses. When I returned with the water, Monty seemed to have composed himself.

'Thanks.' He popped the pill on his tongue. 'The headaches don't last more than a minute, but it's like someone puts my head in a vice and keeps turning the handle.'

I immediately thought of a dozen terminal diseases Monty could have. I was never an optimist where illness was concerned and I worried that Monty wasn't as healthy as I first thought. 'You need to get it checked it out.'

'This helps.'

Monty chewed on an ice cube, setting my teeth on

edge. I grimaced; he may as well be running his nails down a blackboard.

'Hey Mother Hen, don't look so concerned. I promise I'll go and see my doctor. Wow, after all this time you're still looking out for me.'

Monty threw me an exasperated look before he turned his attention to a mural on the ceiling. I couldn't see anything fascinating in the renaissance artwork and I decided to start fishing for clues.

'Don't you miss it?'

Monty furrowed his brows. 'Miss what?'

'London. The eighties. All that freedom, no boundaries, no commitments.'

I knew we mustn't dwell on our past but I couldn't help it. During our three years in the capital we single handedly raised the bar for excess. We blazed the trail.

*We were the news.*

'Don't you remember, we always said if you're not living on the edge make way for someone who is!'

Monty smiled in appreciation of his celebrated phrase.

I babbled on. 'Your American escapade got me thinking…do you remember the end of term ball when you and Charles dressed up as mummies?'

Monty poured himself another large glass of wine before settling back into his seat. The headache had obviously passed but the night in question drew a blank expression.

He crossed his arms behind his head. 'You're right, we had some crazy times. What did they say about the sixties, if you could remember them you weren't there? For me that period of my life was much the same.'

I pulled a quizzical face. 'You never took drugs, but you drank for England'

'Comme ci, comme ça.'

Monty could say anything in French and it would sound believable.

'Well I saw you take a joint once. One puff and you went green, it was hilarious.'

It was obvious Monty couldn't recall his one attempt at getting high but my memories were streaming back like a film projector running out of control. I had to physically reign myself in. There was so much more I wanted to ask him about and I didn't know where to start.

I reached into my inside pocket for the envelope and took out the photographs.

'Look what I found.'

We hunched over the first Polaroid. Monty started laughing first, long and hard and I followed suit. There was Charles in a red top hat, a mass of dreadlocks tumbling underneath, fishnet stockings and stilettos, with a baby's bib covering his privates. Monty held the photo of Charles dressed as Boy George up to the overhead lamp. I studied his face carefully.

*What do you remember that you're not telling me?*

'I can't believe some of the things we…' I stopped in mid-sentence not wanting to appear maudlin. After a short pause I generated sufficient courage to continue. 'What about the party in Baker Street? Come on you must remember that?'

Monty scratched his head.

'Was that at Gordon's? With the stuffed bear and the dentist's chair.'

'No, wrong party.'

Monty grimaced like he had heartburn or bad tooth ache. Then he grabbed my hand. 'I need to share something with you.'

His grip was strong and my fingers tingled.

'My entire life is full of blanks. Not just the odd

evening, whole fucking months.'

He released my hand and I rubbed feeling back into it. I feared I already knew the answer.

'I recall general stuff and sometimes I get a brief flashback, but I'm not able to connect. Not properly. On the odd occasion I do remember something it feels like I'm viewing someone else's life. One specialist I saw diagnosed some form of amnesia.'

*Memory loss*

This was not what I wanted to hear and I deliberated over the cause of his angst. It was a well-known fact Monty never suffered from hangovers, which was surprising in itself considering how much alcohol he consumed. I thought about the tequila, a dormant rugby injury or the lethal gas fire.

Monty leant forward, his hands pressed together.

'I've kept this secret for a long time.' A knot tightened in my stomach. Was it going to be this easy? I doubted it.

'My father was so worried about my reliance on alcohol that he sent me to a French seminary to dry out. Can you imagine that? Me in a bloody seminary; monks and prayer time, meditation, and reams of philosophy.'

Monty raised his eyebrows, like he was expecting me to respond in some way.

He was right. I was primed and about to ask him the million dollar question, but I drew back as I considered the consequences of Monty's lost memory. I thought about the bodyguard in the car with Diana. Trevor Rees-Jones. Was his inability to remember a co-incidence or a monumental cover up? I thought how similar my predicament was to that tragic day in August, the answers tantalisingly close yet perhaps lost forever. Inside, I laughed at the paradox.

'How long were you in this seminary?' I asked.

'Just a week.'

I tried to hide my disbelief. I simply couldn't imagine it.

'Did it help?' I asked casually.

'I think it saved me from myself. If that's not too clichéd. I didn't wake up one morning and find God sitting on the end of my bed or anything religious like that. I just began to realise how much I was missing out on. I learned to live in the present, live each minute, each hour, each day. Afterwards I stopped drinking for a year, it gave me back my perspective on life, but look at me, I went through all that and I'm still the venerable bachelor. Anyway enough of this boring self-help crap.'

I'd been distracted by Monty's confession but I regained my composure.

I searched the archives and retrieved a helix of memories from deep in my sub-conscious. Monty had no idea what I was capable of. His expression pleaded with me to start and he drummed his fingers on the table.

I leant forward, my body trembled with pent up energy. 'We were in demand back then, there seemed to be a party every weekend.'

Monty cracked a sarcastic smile.

'Some of us still are.'

A heavily muscled arm rested gently on my shoulder, like a father imparting wisdom to his son.

'You know what I mean.' But inside I was worried Monty had seen right through me. I wished I still had the magic, but I felt it left me a long time ago.

Monty winked slyly.

'I reckon we could all hit the self-destruct button again if we wanted to. I got a taxi here, so what about another bottle?'

I smiled cheerfully. 'Why not? Charles can get the

next one, if he ever turns up.' I realised it was naïve of me to assume this evening would be light on alcohol. I could get a cab and leave my car overnight if I needed to. I told my wife not to wait up, but I had been prudent with the truth. In fact I had lied about who I was meeting and I had no idea why. She didn't know them.

His face was inches from mine. A grapey sourness to his breath, a musky manly scent. I thought he was going to kiss me but he pulled back at the last moment. I wouldn't have thought it strange if he had. A long time ago we had all been very close. Brothers in arms and like an ache deep in the marrow of my bones, I realised I had missed him more than words or a kiss could say.

For a moment Monty looked perturbed.

I swallowed hard and turned my face away from his, fearful Monty sensed something was up.

*Was I depressed? Was my life that bad?*

I was about to start my story when Monty grabbed my arm. The Monty of old, a twinkle in his eye, animated and eager.

His French accent returned. 'Do you remember Charles and I sold doughnuts on a beach in the South of France? It was all illegal of course. We slept in cardboard boxes up in the dunes and got arrested more times than I can remember for selling food without a permit. It was a pretty depraved time, we drank Pastis for breakfast…we…' He looked embarrassed.

I knew what he was about to say, but I didn't interrupt.

He lowered his voice. 'We stole food from restaurant tables so we didn't go hungry.'

'See, there are still some things you can remember.' I was relieved his hard drive hadn't been completely wiped clean.'

Monty stopped and rubbed his face. A low groan escaped his lips.

I thought there was more to come but I didn't push him, I just nodded knowingly. I remembered the stories from Le Lavendou; it was a crazy time for everyone.

Charles had been at his most promiscuous and fucked himself stupid with anything that moved. He made numerous visits to a clinic when he got back and I remembered the lurid details of his invasive treatment made me squirm.

Monty slowly lowered his hands to the table.

'You never came did you? Always something better

to do?' Monty touched his nose with his finger as though he knew some well-kept secret.

My memory bank was fizzing. I recalled the mahogany tans, the tight Speedos and battered sun hats. Charles and Monty had always spent more time together the Public School bond right to the very end. I shivered; my grave had been walked on again. Or John's had.

Although his last remark unsettled me I ignored his subtle dig and changed tack.

'You know I went to visit Charles once. I took the train down to St Raphael and met him at a beach club. He'd been working as a commis chef for the entire summer. He always got the lucky breaks.'

Monty's eyes glazed over. 'Club Tropicana,' he repeated wistfully.

'Can you believe he found somewhere to work called that?'

Monty shook his head knowingly. 'It could only happen to Charles.'

I arrived the day he was packing up to come home. After two days travelling I ended up on a deserted beach with nowhere to stay. Charles of course didn't give a toss. There were no mobile phones back then and occasionally cock-ups like that happened; you just had to shrug your shoulders and get on with it. I had no alternative but to walk up to the coastal road and hitch-hike back towards civilisation. I hadn't walked more than a hundred yards along that dusty road when my luck changed. A VW Combi sped past, braked and pulled over. I certainly had a lucky guardian ride along with me that day because in the front seats were two German girls from Berlin, touring Europe. We ended up in St Tropez and I spent the next week sleeping with both of them on an air mattress under the stars.

Monty whistled through his front teeth.

'They should have bottled what you had back then. '

Monty was right. Even though I had a steady girlfriend I hadn't been very monogamous. Charles and I were in competition and we kept our conquests in a small note book. We were young, good looking and horny and the pages filled quickly; girls were no more than a notch in the headboard. Looking back I wasn't very proud of my behaviour. Monty was different, like Stephen Fry or Jeeves and Wooster, girls hung on his every word and there was one in particular who stepped out with him more than once. Few questioned his sexuality because he didn't have a feminine bone in his body, he was just indifferent. He was just Monty.

'Do you have anyone now?' I asked tentatively. I felt like I was prying.

'No. I live alone in a rented cottage in deepest darkest Surrey. I had a girlfriend in Cambodia once, but it didn't work out.' His tone was all of a sudden quiet and unconvincing. For some strange reason I wasn't sure I believed him. I attempted to hide my surprise behind a smile. I never imagined Monty would end up living on his own.

For a moment he appeared pre-occupied, glum even. I hid my concern and tried to sound upbeat. 'I'm sorry. Plenty more fish in the sea.'

He shrugged. 'I'm sure there are, but I ask myself whether I need a partner. The seminary taught me solitude. I like being on my own, I've grown selfish.'

Like Charles, his gregarious nature was tempered by blinkered vision and I reflected that Public School and his domineering mother had a lot to answer for. I couldn't ever imagine being on my own, the voices in my head would finish me off.

'Everyone needs somebody Monty.'

I studied him closely and something with which he seemed to be burdened, lifted.

He punched my arm and winked. 'Ignore me, I'm being morose and I have no reason to be. Go on, get on with your story, you know I'm only jealous of all your womanising.'

Although looking back now I wasn't sure I had any of it right.

# FANCY DRESS

We moved to Pimlico in the spring of 1982. After four months of freezing our nuts off in W14, Charles instructed me to find somewhere within walking distance of College. I didn't think my negotiating skills were any better than the other two, but it was evident they couldn't be bothered with the hum drum banality of flat hunting.

Charles knew that if I smiled sweetly enough at the agent we would get a good deal. I found a small agency near Vauxhall Bridge Road. Ironically it was run by an anxious woman with thinning hair and impetigo, who was about as attractive as a rat with scabies. She wasn't quite the vision of loveliness I had previously imagined over the phone.

Luckily she took a shine to me and I went to look at 89A, a small, two bedroom basement flat in one of the white Regency villas on Winchester Street. The streets were well-kept, wide and tree-lined, very different from W14. The house number was etched into one of the brilliant white pillars, while at street level a wrought iron swing gate led down steep steps to our front door, which had an ingenious spy hole.

The agent promised me a well-kept flat with period features but the furniture was dark and sombre and the heavy drapes made it feel slightly claustrophobic. There was little natural light in the front bedroom and the ornate double bed rattled noisily whenever Charles entertained. The rear bedroom flooded whenever it rained due to a decrepit damp course but the kitchen was bright and modern, and most importantly for the summer months it allowed access to the courtyard garden. Charles and Monty never saw the interior until we moved in, but I was quietly satisfied; I knew it ticked all the boxes for entertaining.

Charles ignored the stuffy Dickensian furnishings. 'At least it has central heating and the garden is perfect for dinner parties,' he announced as he dumped his bags in the front bedroom.

I had gone up in the world. Winchester Street was one of the many roads that ran parallel to the Embankment. Four-storey terraced houses that now must be worth millions. I said yes on the spot and arranged a date for keys to be collected and our deposit to be paid. It was that easy, I don't think the agency even asked for references. We used 89A as our base until we left

College, until that final night at Baz and Annie's.

I shot my cuffs. Monty watched me closely and I realised I had been imitating his exact habit for years. His large soulful eyes fixed intently on mine. Eyes that seemed to alter in colour dependent on his mood. Tonight, unexpectedly, they said entertain me.

'Come on then, tell me about this great party I was at.'

I closed my eyes. I saw the invitation propped up on our dusty mantelpiece. I viewed it all like it was yesterday and it triggered a helter skelter of memories. It was around the time Prince William was born and in the surrounding streets bunting and flags hung from balconies and windows. Charles and Monty had reputations to protect after the Mummy episode and they deliberated for ages about their costumes. I had no such worries. I went as Mad Max. Sadly I wasn't quite a Mel Gibson look alike, but I had the vintage biker's jacket and leather trousers. Max was my hero and his road movies were revered by us all.

Charles created a leg brace for me, a magnificent structure which consisted of two metal splints held in place by segments of old bicycle tube. The top tube attached to my knee, while the bottom rode under the sole of my right boot. Scrap-yard design was his thing; he could make anything from items that the rest of us thought worthless. It was an impressive piece of engineering and I loved the way the splint made me walk with an authentic limp.

I looked across at Monty, he had his eyes shut and I sensed he was trying to take in my over dose of nostalgia, although I wasn't sure he remembered these events with any clarity. Charles went as Fred Flintstone. He wrapped an old rug round his body that left nothing to the imagination. The Pimlico caveman needed a club and Charles fashioned one out of old newspaper and brown masking tape. It was quite an effective weapon. Monty was last to appear, dressed in full black tails, dress shirt and bow tie, with a white towel fastened round his crotch, like a nappy. He made an excellent Lord Greystoke.

We looked like rejects from a bizarre film audition and I watched pedestrians stop and point as we walked to the bus stop. I told Monty it reminded me of the Mummy episode where he and Charles wrapped themselves head to toe in strips of old yellow sheets. One with a shuttlecock shoved down his pants, the other with papier-maché boobs. The disguises were so good that no-one ever knew who was under the bandages that night.

'I vaguely remember the Mummy episode now,' Monty snorted, snapping apart a pistachio nut.

By the time we got to the party it was in full swing, although the film star theme seemed open to interpretation. The hosts knew Charles and Monty from the south of France and the girls immediately whisked them off to dance. Charles as usual was his loud, brash self and within a short time he was showing everyone what a caveman had underneath his rug! I remember thinking what drives a girl to want to dance with a guy in such a smelly outfit.

I stopped talking for a moment and looked across the table at Monty. His forehead was peppered with beads of sweat. It was a warm spring evening and either my nerves had got the better of me or the air conditioning in the bar had stopped working, because my shirt had damp patches under my arms.

Monty choked on his wine 'God he always had his cock out. Charles and his cock!'

Tears streamed from his eyes and people turned self-consciously to see if the joke was on them. Monty produced a white handkerchief from his pocket. It was monogrammed, neatly folded and pristine, a handkerchief from a different time. He gently dabbed his forehead with it. The earlier awkwardness had disappeared, although I'm sure we were both aware important things remained unsaid between us.

'Go on, your memory is unbelievable, are you sure you're not making this up.'

'No, I discovered I have a special gift when it comes to remembering. '

Monty looked around suspiciously as though we were entering into some sort of illicit drug deal.

'I see, a gift. I'm intrigued.'

I felt myself blush. I felt like I was opening up my soul.

'A secret talent?' he whispered.

'It's not really. I read up about it, some professor published a study on it. Eidetic recall they call it. It's not that uncommon.' I couldn't hold it in any longer. 'It's going to help me, because I've started to write a book,' I gushed.

I waited for him to shoot me down in flames. It

happened frequently to me at the moment. But Monty looked suitably impressed.

He patted my back.

'I need to do something different with my life,' I said.

'Good lad, I always said to Charles you had a vivid imagination. Well we have something in common then. I am surrounded by books at home, sometimes I can't even climb into bed. I read far too much, it's a symptom of living alone but if you need a mate to critique any of it you know where to come.'

I didn't remember Monty reading for pleasure. I was taken aback.

Monty clapped his hands together. 'I'm envious. You know what that's a brave move, just make sure you stick at it. They say it's a marathon not a sprint, but I'm in no doubt someone as tenacious as you will be successful. I look forward to reading the reviews, and make sure I'm invited to the press launch.'

I raised my glass. 'You'll be the first.' A surge of pride welled up inside. I wished my own family felt the same.

Monty spread his arms along the banquette.

'What's it going to be about?'

I wasn't prepared for any prying questions and my response sounded unconvincing. 'People and places, something mysterious.'

Monty nodded. 'Charles will take the piss, you know that don't you?'

I knew how black-and-white things were for Charles and I wished I hadn't mentioned it. With him it was all about making a fast buck and I knew he wouldn't be so accommodating with his views.

'So who else was at this party? Brocky, Niels any of the Radley crowd?'

'No, none of them. Do you remember Chris? He was there.'

Chris had a giraffe like neck. He bore little resemblance to his hero Clint Eastwood, even though he was over six feet tall, wearing a poncho and cowboy boots. Some people just didn't look like the stars they were imitating I thought.

I singled out two girls that night. They both wore heavy black make up, chain's and jet black Cleopatra wigs. I wasn't sure if they were dressed as Goths or Vampires, in the end I don't think it mattered which, they were dressed to kill. I stood nearby and stamped my leg a few times to authenticate my rugged image. They didn't seem put off so I moved in.

Charles and I were always in competition back then, and I remember thinking, if I could pull this off it was going in the book, underlined, in red. However, after a short period of flirtation it appeared these girls had been playing me all along. They plainly saw me in a completely different light. I leant across and whispered in Monty's ear. Speaking the words out loud seemed too much to bear.

Monty looked amused and his voice echoed off the walls of the alcove.

'The biker from the Village People, seriously?'

Monty chortled, and snorted. Tears ran down his face. People standing nearby turned to see what all the fuss was about. I raised my eyes to the heavens. The story seemed ridiculous even now.

It turned out the girls only had eyes and tongues for each other and after my rebuttal I made a hasty exit. I set about finding my flatmates and putting some distance between me and the girls, which was difficult because the flat was quite small. I found Charles in a bedroom lying between the legs of a blonde. His bare arse was unmistakable, it was the stuff of legends. I realised I had little chance of any sympathy so I sat myself down in a chair and did what he had done countless times to me: be very bloody annoying.

Monty shook his head in disbelief.

'You had a conversation with Charles while he was shagging?'

'Pretty much.' It wasn't the first or last time I had been up close and personal with Charles while he was in action.

'So where was I when this little tête-á-tête took place?'

'I found you lying in a bath with an empty scotch bottle by your side. I thought you were dead.'

Monty thumped his chest like a gladiator. 'It would take more than a bottle of scotch.'

'I'm so relieved you made it here tonight,' I said earnestly, quelling the urge to hug him again.

Monty clapped his hands together. 'What was that great line you said in the cab when I kept asking where Charles was?'

'Caveman doing what a caveman does best.'

'Now that's funny.'

'It's how it happened. Trust me.'

'Did I seriously get on a bus to Baker Street in a nappy? God I wish I could remember…'

'You were there, believe me.'

The bar was filling up and I tapped my watch. Monty shrugged his shoulders and held out his wine glass. I tried to see behind the mask. It was patently obvious we were sparring with each other, the early exchanges probing but ineffective. What other secrets had we kept from each other? We savoured the wine and waited for the prodigal son to arrive, but unspoken questions hung between us like dark shadows.

# CHARLES

An attractive woman standing nearby cursed under her breath as a hunched figure barged his way towards our table. We both turned. Our jaws dropped.

'Charles? Jesus!'

He forced his twisted features into a broad grin.

'Hello boys, just like old times eh!'

I tried to conceal my shock by being flippant. 'You mean you arriving late.'

He ran a hand over my buzz cut.

'What happened to you, join the army?' Charles always asked rhetorical questions, although part of me thought he was being serious.

His right arm was in a sling; the plaster cast matched his pink shirt. A black eye patch covered one eye. If he'd come out of the wartime trenches he wouldn't have looked out of place. It was the same Charles though and his good eye still sparkled with mischief. I nudged Monty. I was unsure whether to laugh or lend a hand to our stricken friend.

In the end I stood up. 'Jesus, what happened…? You look one hell of a mess by the way.'

Our recent communications had been by text. Charles had simply confirmed the time and place of our meeting. No more, no less.

Charles gritted his teeth. 'You should see the other guy.'

Monty shuffled round the booth and gestured for Charles to sit.

'Asseyez-vous Charles.'

His Gallic accent purposely thick and nasal, before he switched effortlessly back to upper class English. 'Well if you're anything to go by old man I presume the other guy's dead.'

Charles lowered himself gingerly onto the seat 'It's all my fault.'

Monty and I were astonished. Nothing had ever been Charles fault, he was the archetypal politician.

Charles carved some turns in the air with his good arm.

'Put simply my good friends, I fell head first onto an unforgiving rock.'

'A rock? Right.'

Charles fiddled with the gauze beneath his eye patch; the area around it was black, puffy and bruised. 'Listen, it's the truth.'

*The truth.*

'I fell down a steep couloir, that's all. No-one died,' he said, manoeuvring himself carefully into the booth next to me.

*No-one died.*

'Sorry. You – were – up - a – mountain? Skiing?' I spoke each word very slowly.

Charles imitated my speech pattern. 'Yes. That - is - what - one - does - up - a - mountain, or have you forgotten?'

I looked at Monty. He held his hand up. He knew intuitively what I was about to say. Instead I tempered my reply with satire.

'Unusual for a man of your ability, to fall.' My words belied the fact that I found the whole conversation a little fucking off–piste itself. The man was reckless and as usual the whole Charles charade was a total spectacle. His good eye twitched but he didn't rise to the bait.

'Ouch.' His face winced as he knocked his thumb on the edge of the table.

Charles reached into a pocket with his good hand. 'Do you want to see the photographs the surgeon took?'

I grimaced. I wasn't good with injuries, either my own or someone else's.

'No I don't want to see any photographs and stop lifting your eye patch.' I began to feel queasy and I slugged back some of Monty's water.

Charles put his phone back in his pocket. 'Bloody thumb, still lucky to have it, although the surgeon reckons I'll get most of the mobility back. At least I'll still be able to wank.'

A woman near us turned and scrutinised him. Charles leered back. Typical Charles, still sensational and attention grabbing.

I held the bottle of wine aloft. 'I'm glad it still works, do you want a drink?'

'I probably shouldn't…I'm on extra strong pain killers at the moment but if it stops this damn throbbing…' He was almost shouting. He was as loud as ever.

'Here have some wine.'

I looked at him, really looked at him and tried to fathom how he had done this with his brother lying on a slab in a West London mortuary. The man was a lunatic. Was he going to mention his twin?

Charles sensed I was staring at him. He reached for the bottle and turned his attention to the wine label.

'What is it, anything good?'

Charles' appreciation of wine always increased significantly if someone else was buying.

'Sancerre, single vineyard.'

'Excellent, I don't want any of that new world crap from South America. It's only fit for fish and chips. Bloody vinegar all of it.'

I poured him half a glass. He gestured for me to keep pouring.

Monty leaned forward. 'Come on put us out of our misery, tell us exactly what happened.' His tone was even and fatherly. It was like he was talking to a stubborn child. I hoped I got the chance to ask Charles some leading questions of my own when the opportunity arose because I was not relying on Monty.

I first met Charles in our smoke filled refectory. He was sitting alone, dabbing a moistened finger into a plastic cup filled with sugar. Sugar and butter his staple diet. It was a few weeks into the autumn term and our class remained one short. Charles, it turned out, had misplaced the letter with the course dates on and he was hunched over a pile of forms. I think he was squeezing out another couple of weeks' wages at the John Howard Hotel where he was working. He was always careful where money was concerned, unlike Monty and I. Ironically he was injured that day too. He hobbled into our lecture on crutches wearing a pair of red and white striped trousers and a slipper on his left foot, and I mistakenly thought he was terribly radical and hip. Fashion was undergoing a bit of an identity crisis at the time and don't ask me how I made the connection, but his slipper reminded me bizarrely of Michael Jackson's lone white glove. It turned out an in-growing toenail was the cause and when I reminded him of it this evening he continued to dispute it and said I'd made the whole story up.

Towards the end of the first term I was taken by Charles and Monty to the Three Kings next to West Kensington tube station. They said it was a matter of great importance. I should tell no-one. I should speak to no-one. I thought it all sounded a bit cloak and dagger and I wondered what dark secret they were about to bestow on me.

Monty let Charles do the talking. The Italian waiter

who shared the flat with them was finally moving out and I was being offered his bed. If I wanted to live with them of course. Did I want to? Did I ever! This was all my Christmases rolled into one. The interview process involved copious amounts of Grolsch beer and pork scratchings, as they fired questions at me like the Spanish Inquisition.

'What school did I go to?'

'What did my Father do?'

'Did I ski?'

'Did I like Scotch?'

'Could I rustle up a cheap meal for three, for under a quid?'

'Did I have access to a washing machine when I went home?'

'Did I have a credit card?'

Well the warning signs were there all along. I felt like l was being groomed for a domestic position and I was right.

I passed the selection process with flying colours. I - was - in. I never asked what became of the Italian waiter; for all I cared, they could have murdered him, chopped him into little pieces and buried him in the garden.

Within a week and amidst much excitement I packed my most precious possessions into an unroadworthy, battered orange Beetle and left home for good.

Almost immediately I received my first valuable survival lesson. In the miniscule kitchen with the two-ringed electric cooker, Charles taught me the necessary skills required to cook our staple diet of sausages, lumpy mash and steamed green cabbage. A skill that luckily I have no need for now. Over the years the tiered saucepan system we created had a few imitators but I like to think we influenced the art of vertical cooking

Charles was dyslexic. It wasn't until he'd been thrown out of a couple of lectures, due to his violent fits of temper, that a valid explanation materialised for his erratic behaviour. It was a time when no-one understood dyslexia and even his parents thought he was a lost cause academically, so they packed him off to a Public School for challenged pupils somewhere in Dorset. Here he excelled in hockey and earned a reputation as a formidable and down-right dangerous goalkeeper. His real passions however lay elsewhere: in rugby, which he played moderately well, shagging, and his forte for taking things apart and putting them back together again.

Dyslexia took away his ability to read and spell but gave him an incredible engineering mind.

Charles and John were non-identical. I was told fraternal twins was the correct medical term. As they grew up it soon became apparent they were cut from entirely different cloth. John excelled at Tiffin School and had offers from Oxford. He had a reputation as a fearsome negotiator but someone who was fair and exuded empathy, quite different from Charles. Compassion and sympathy didn't exist in Charles' world, it was all about me, me, me. The boys met up occasionally during the holidays when their mother prepared lavish Sunday roasts at their Surrey mansion. This tradition continued well into their twenties and Monty and I were invited a couple of times, but for me this formal dining experience was more ordeal than enjoyment and the scrutiny one came under seemed out of kilter with my semi-detached roots.

Like most boys who had spent their formative years at boarding school, Charles was fiercely independent and a complete chauvinist. He was a staunch Conservative, politically active and soon became chairman of the student Union. He was a tad over six feet, with blonde hair and blue eyes which made him look a little Aryan; thank God he didn't exhibit any other Nazi tendencies! Imagine Alan B'stard and you have Charles down to a tee.

He was extremely fond of showing everyone his flaccid penis, which, though it grieves me to admit, was above the average. One lingering memory I have of Charles was returning to the flat after a meal with a new girlfriend and finding him in the middle of the living room, in his underpants, surrounded by bike parts and a fish and chip supper. He grunted a 'hello' and then resumed his bike maintenance, whilst dipping horribly greasy fingers into the fish and chip paper. The room looked like a garage and smelt of vinegar and WD40.

'I wasn't expecting you back?' he mumbled through a mouthful of chips.

My date for the evening took one look at Charles and his deconstructed bike and left.

His future dreams were shaped around life as a Lord in a small castle or a folly, with a flagpole in the garden where he could, run up the Union Jack or fly his family's coat of arms. He had the perfect ally in Monty but I never felt comfortable with all that macho, prop forward machismo.

'Far too in touch with your feminine side,' Charles would say whenever he saw me trying to bring order to our lives. In secret I think he wished he could have been a little bit more like me. I did find small chinks in his armour and witnessed occasional moments of tenderness and concern, like the time he lay with me on my bed after my parents had divorced, but they were fleeting and not seen by everyone. I recalled female opinions being split fifty-fifty as to whether he was a good catch or just a pain in the arse, but despite all his bad traits he had a big heart and was an incredibly loyal friend. Monty and I accepted that we would always play second fiddle and were happy to let him believe he was King. Well King of the bedroom. 'It's good to be King,' Charles would say whenever he wanted to convey his superiority.

I almost expected him to break off from his story, fix us with his steely eye and say those exact words now. Instead he caught us both off guard and described meticulously a glorious day in the Alps, where the mountain peaks hovered, as if suspended above the clouds. Where the only sound you heard was your own blood pumping in your ears and the occasional snowfall from a conifer. It brought it all crashing back to me. It's what we used to live for and I realised how much I missed it.

'It's what I live for and I spend a lot of time and money doing it. Only now I love the climb up as much as the descent.' He wagged an index finger at us.

'Just don't tell the wife.'

I hoped John had seen enough of those near perfect blue sky days before he died. I really hoped he had.

'Thanks for the travel notes,' I replied sarcastically.

Charles paused for effect.

'What a day we had had up 'til then. It was my turn to navigate a steep, narrow gully. My guide waited at the bottom. I should have been paying attention but I wasn't and I missed his warning.'

'Was he Welsh?' Monty enquired politely. Charles had possibly the worst French accent anyone had ever heard.

Charles sneered. It implied that we were to shut the fuck up and listen.

'He was French. Well actually he's Swiss.'

'Swiss French or Swiss German?' I asked.

A look of disdain followed.

'Hey just kidding.' I felt it was time to back off with the wisecracks.

'It doesn't matter where he was born. Anyway the next thing I knew I was somersaulting down the slope head first. I remember thinking "Oh shit, this is going to hurt!" and I raised my arms to protect my head. No helmet you see. My skis came off and I braced myself for a collision. I hadn't fallen that far but I hit the rock hard, my shoulder and arm taking the full brunt. I thought well at least it wasn't my head; worst scenario broken arm, dislocated shoulder. I winced as I imagined the brutal forces involved.

'One of my poles caught me in the eye and when I tried to pick up one of my skis I found I couldn't. That's when I took my glove off.'

I swallowed hard.

Charles laughed. 'My thumb was bloody missing.'

Monty peered closely at the swollen, fleshy appendage poking out of the plaster. 'Did they build you a bionic one?'

I reflected that Monty must be immune to gouges, cuts and breaks after his antics on the rugby field.

Charles continued. 'The surgeon said it was the worst

dislocation he had ever seen.'

I turned away. I didn't want look too closely at the injury. I experienced a rush of nausea and rapidly lost interest in the wine bar's menu. Charles continued with his story, oblivious to my inner suffering.

'I held my pole up to signify I was injured and my guide climbed up to me. We had three attempts to push my thumb back into place. It was excruciatingly painful and even my ice cool guide looked a little green round the gills. After two or three attempts to get a signal he got through to the air ambulance. Those guys are like International Rescue and they honestly saved my life.'

I hummed the memorable theme tune.

Charles sneered and did a puppet impersonation with his one good arm. 'Very funny...I was close to blacking out and my guide began to look more and more concerned, a bit like you two now. I had blurred vision and I found out later I had a detached retina in my right eye. My external injuries were not life threatening but the guide was worried I might have an internal bleed.'

I watched Charles check himself out in a mirror. He was clearly enjoying himself. 'I couldn't see the helicopter at first because my eyes were full of snow and grit, but I could hear the rotors getting closer.'

'How long did it take to get to you?' Monty asked.

'Ten minutes, that's all. I have to pay a vast amount in insurance cover so I expect the best, but even I was relieved when the helicopter appeared overhead and I knew I was going to make it off the mountain. The pilot said they could winch me off and I'd be in a Zurich hospital in 15 minutes.'

Charles chopped the air with his good hand.

'Needless to say I declined. '

Monty slapped his forehead. 'Charles. What! Are you fucking mad?'

'Listen, I read about this guy who was winched off at exactly the same height as me, 3,000 metres. On his way to hospital he suffered terrible frost bite. You just hang in a harness, swinging below the helicopter, open to the elements.'

I raised my eyes to the ceiling. Still bloody-minded and stubborn, but he had a point I thought.

'One option was to walk down, like the guy with the busted leg in Vertical Limit, but the slope was very steep and treacherous, and it would have been a long walk. We needed a Plan B and quickly. The pilot must have heard our thoughts because just as we were about to give up he highlighted a small flat boulder about 20 metres up to our left. I would have climbed up a tree if I'd had to. Once I was lying on the boulder the pilot touched down right beside me, the skid was so close I could touch the rail with my hand.'

Charles paused and sipped his wine.

'With a little help from a medic I climbed aboard. Once we'd landed at the hospital I was taken immediately to see the triage nurse. My stomach looked like it was going to burst and I was whisked straight into theatre.'

'You're bloody lucky to be alive,' Monty said.

Charles grinned. 'You could say that.'

'They operated on my ruptured bowel immediately. The internal bleeding stopped and I was off the critical list, but I had to wait until I got back to Shrewsbury to have my thumb rebuilt. The surgeon was a business colleague and at first he feared I might lose my thumb. I still don't know what the movement will be like when the screws come out, but he did a good job. It still hurts like buggery though.'

Charles smiled and then grimaced, the searing pain

obvious. He was one tough old sod but I struggled to put this whole conversation into context. It was all daring dramatic stuff but surely he didn't come here tonight simply to recall his own near-death experience.

Instead Charles bulldozered on, he never dwelt on his past and I sensed he was clearly avoiding the subject of his brother's death. I wanted to ask him about that fateful night in Battersea, I wanted to ask him about everything but something stopped me. He rarely let his guard down and the voice in my head told me to tread very carefully.

## LUCY AND THE ARAB

Charles was wounded but not for one second did he dwell on his misfortune and a familiar veil of acceptance enveloped Monty and me. Charles had always rejected sympathy and never gave any in return. I reflected that nothing much had changed. Charles was still Charles. At least tonight, he had a decent excuse for being late. He ordered a pitcher of Margherita from a passing waitress. I observed his coy manner purely reserved for communications with the opposite sex, the brief exchange a thirty second interview to sleep with him.

Charles caressed my head with his good hand; it was his way of dispensing affection. He had a certain tenderness for a man who led a rugged outdoor life and for some strange reason I imagined his many lovers writhing under his delicate touch. He pinched my cheek. 'No wonder those College girls wanted to mother you.'

I hastily shook the idea from my mind, clearing the image of Charles caught 'in flagrante'. However I knew which direction he was going with this.

Charles pressed a finger to the side of his forehead.

'What was her name?'

Monty looked around blankly.

'Dark hair, in the year above.' Charles loved to talk about women and sex, it didn't matter who was doing it, or to whom, he just had to talk about it.

'Lucy,' I added.

Charles turned to Monty and leered. 'Do you remember Lucy?' Charles did his best with his one good hand to accentuate an ample bosom.

Sadly, a grey mist had descended on Monty again.

Monty raised a palm to his mouth and yawned in the manner of someone who was bored. 'Ben's conquests. Remind me, there were so many.'

I couldn't explain it. In my early twenties women of all ages were drawn to me, it was an invisible magnetic force and something over which I had absolutely no control.

*Conquest*s.

It was such a horrible word I thought. More in line with raping and pillaging than anything passionate and tender.

'She was the one with the Arabic boyfriend,' I explained.

Charles was loosening up. 'Come on Ben remind us

what happened with juicy Lucy. She was a third year wasn't she?'

The film spool started rolling in my head once more. At the end of each term the whole year were split into groups and invited to host a drinks party. The budgets were generous and the cocktail making, while enthusiastic, sometimes crossed the line between racy and downright lethal. The only food on offer were the plentiful segments of fruit floating in the large silver cauldrons and it wasn't surprising that some less experienced, and possibly more sensible, students never made it to the second venue. I met Lucy in a pub after a cocktail party.

The Green-Coat Boy was not your typical student watering hole; it had a long bar running the length of one wall and the interior was cosmopolitan, rather than spit and sawdust. It didn't quite have the kudos of the White Horse and Pucci Pizza in Kong's Road at Parsons Green but it was the closest decent pub to College.

'Well stop daydreaming, was she a third year?'

I acquiesced. 'Yes she was.'

Charles grinned. 'I bet old Price is dead now. He'll be remembered for his parties though. I doubt the local residents had ever seen so many drunken students stumbling around Vincent Square at dusk.'

Price was one of our wine lecturers, ruddy cheeks, a limp and comb over.

I slumped against the banquette. 'Do you want to tell this story or shall I?'

Charles fiddled self-consciously with his eye patch. I couldn't help thinking he would have made an excellent Lord Nelson.

'Yes. Sorry I'll stop interrupting.'

Charles zipped his mouth shut with two unbound long fingers, but I knew he wouldn't be able to keep quiet for long.

Lucy was dark haired, voluptuous with a hint of something sultry in her veins. She was self-assured and confident and after manoeuvring me into an empty alcove, I spent most of the evening smothered between her impressive breasts. Lucy was experienced and knew exactly what she wanted and how to get it.

When we finally left the pub she casually invited me back to her house, she said it was only a few stops on the Central Line. It was actually in Perivale, a million miles from SW1 and the tube journey seemed to go on forever.

*Girls and geography.*

It soon became apparent she didn't live alone. Her girlfriend very politely disappeared when she realised three was a crowd. Lucy made something that resembled coffee and we chatted for a bit before I went upstairs and promptly fell asleep in the spare bedroom. Lucy must have thought I was boorish and probably wondered why I had lost interest in her! I hadn't, I was just exhausted.

Sometime later I sensed a presence in my room. I felt a hand on my shoulder, hot breath and a familiar intoxicating fragrance. I opened my eyes and Lucy was sitting on the edge of the bed, naked. I remembered she smelt musky, on heat.

'I ended up in her double bed. Enough said,' I replied.

Monty and Charles watched me like two dogs waiting for a treat. It clearly wasn't enough detail for Charles.

'Come on you tease, remind us exactly what happened.'

'What, you mean all the kinky stuff?' I added, just to goad him.

Charles banged his good hand on the table. 'No, you know what I mean.'

Even though it was well over two decades ago I felt

like I was back in Lucy's bed. We shared a joint afterwards. I was looking forward to a few hours of well-earned sleep when she announced quite calmly that it was probably best if I left. It took a while for her words to sink in. Why did she want me to leave? She dropped the bombshell. She had a boyfriend. She was worried he might come back. As an afterthought she told me he was Arabic. I was petrified and conjured up all manner of gory scenarios where he returns home to find me in bed with his girl.

Charles simulated knife torture to my nether regions.

'Did you sleep with her again?' Monty asked.

'No, we never even spoke. I bet I wasn't the first guy she'd invited back while he was away.'

Charles adjusted his eye patch.

'So what if she did, it was all clean harmless fun, nobody got hurt, life moves on. You can't keep being a sentimental softy. You need to get some balls.'

I tried to defend myself. 'Harmless! Hardly. I could have been mutilated in my sleep.'

Charles shrugged his shoulders and started banging on to Monty about taking shares in a gold mine in Africa. It was thoroughly boring crap. Meanwhile nostalgia was running through my veins and I began to revisit some of my relationships. My list of lovers grew ever longer and I tried to put the faces in some sort of sequence: it was quite a task.

Charles prodded me with his good hand; he didn't like it if you weren't paying attention to him.

'Hey pretty boy, you look like you're off with the fairies.'

I grunted a response. The list still needed some work before it was completed. A number of faces remained frustratingly nameless and I squeezed every ounce out of my cerebral neurons to complete the task before Charles realised I was not completely in the present.

I caught his eye.

'No I'm good, I'm listening'.

Which of course I wasn't; I had drifted back to the neat tree-lined streets of Pimlico in the eighties and to be brutally honest, I wasn't sure I was the right demographic for his sales pitch.

I began to recall the unparalleled sex life of my early twenties and tried to fathom why I had been so popular. Most people weren't aware that underneath all the self-absorbed posturing I was a complex character, a daydreamer and fantasist I suppose. After my parents divorced I was driven by an innate desire to be liked, but instead I became easily bored I pursued a devil-may-care attitude to my early relationships. I was clearly desperate to find something I was good at, I just never thought it would be anything as simple as becoming a grand master in the art of giving pleasure. The big 'O.'

Surely I must have had something more extraordinary going for me than that? I reflected on my chief attributes, my 'Je ne sais quoi', but it soon became apparent after a spell of soul searching, I hadn't. I was just a normal guy. I certainly had no decent chat-up lines and I never mapped out a seduction plan. I was just a good listener and to this day many of my sexual encounters remained a complete mystery to me, like my night with Lucy for example.

I always imagined I was in control of these steamy liaisons but now I suddenly saw them differently. It was a moment of enlightenment: I never decided who I slept with; they did. This rationale came as a bit of a shock and I started laughing. It was only meant to be internalised, but my amusement sneaked out.

'What's so funny?' Charles enquired, as he demanded

a clean glass from a waitress in an even shorter skirt.

I felt like I had been caught with my hands in the till. 'Nothing, I was just thinking about a little trick Lucy taught me,' I lied. I didn't want to be drawn on the real reason for my outburst. Charles wouldn't get it. Unfortunately the spotlight was directed at me once again.

'Ben, the truth please. Did it involve ice cubes?'

I sighed. 'No. Why are you so fucking obsessed with ice cubes?' The subject of ice cubes amused Charles no end and he waved his plaster cast around in a dangerous manner, nearly hitting a light fitting.

Ice cubes and foreplay. I never quite understood who was supposed to do what with them and decided it was probably too late to find out now, although I was desperately in need of some now (ice cubes not foreplay). It was unbearably hot in the bar and I felt a trickle of sweat run down my side. While Charles demonstrated something wicked to Monty I slipped out of my jacket, placed it on the shelf behind me and undid a couple of buttons on my shirt.

'Tell us how sexually depraved she was, or I'm going to bore you with a few shots of me up to my chest in

Swiss powder. Where's my bloody phone?'

While Charles searched for his sleek black phone I travelled back in time again.

Our joint passion had been snow skiing, always had been, always would be. Sadly, I had only taken our own children twice, because as the recession bit deeply into our pockets, the money dried up and I just couldn't afford two holidays a year. It had been different when I had a College grant and a small inheritance to live off. Charles and Monty had skied from an early age just like their fathers, both of whom I discovered had been posted to Austria shortly after the war. In London, mid-December heralded the start of another season, boots came down from the loft, skis were waxed and the indigenous population of Chelsea headed for the French Alps. In hindsight I don't think we would have had the same relationship if we hadn't shared the thrills and spills of the mountains.

My family had high expectations of me reaching the pinnacle of some sport or other. I had a natural flair; however, most of my sporting dreams were dashed by two contributing factors: a lack of transport (my mother didn't drive) and my father's continual migration to the nearest pub. Around that time, I acknowledged my under-achievement as the reason for countless recurring dreams where I scored the winning goal or hit the winning runs for my club or country. I was a frustrated sportsman and the dreams continued for much of my adult life.

In my early twenties I desperately wanted to stand out, so I grew my hair long. Charles and Monty detested my attempt at a pony tail and continually threatened to cut it off while I slept. There followed a few embarrassing episodes where I was propositioned in squares and parks, and even at a tennis tournament. Was I confused sexually? I don't think so. Men's bits certainly didn't hold the same attraction as women's. I just think for a while I gave out the wrong signals. Thankfully, I never succumbed, although if I had experimented just once I don't think Charles would have been the least bit surprised.

In a corner of the wine bar, a jazz duo began a soothing rendition of a Cole Porter classic. It triggered a powerful remembrance in Charles and for some unknown reason he recalled the IRA bombing of Horse Guards Parade and Regent's Park. We were drinking in a pub behind Harrods when the first nail-bomb exploded and we rushed outside to see plumes of black smoke rising above the famous building. We watched the terrifying events unfold as on a black and white TV, as newsflashes revealed the callous atrocities that had been committed by the IRA. Afterwards we found a nearby phone box and phoned our anxious parents to let them know we were alive and well. Monty had the military in his bloodline and even though the events of that day were dwarfed by the terrorist attacks on 9/11 and 7/7 he stood up and proposed a toast to the soldiers who had died on that darkest of days.

I continued to drift between the past and the present, and only heard snippets of the next conversation as Charles tried again to convince Monty to invest some part of his future inheritance in his new business venture. He had a blueprint for a management company that would revolutionise the mining industry, cutting costs and corruption.

Charles was in full sales mode and I could see Monty physically wilt under the onslaught. From my own perspective it all sounded completely bonkers and I imagined Charles' shackled body appearing on News at

Ten, as his fellow directors acquiesced to the demands of balaclava-clad terrorists and secured his release, with or without his thumbs. I'm positive Monty hadn't understood a garbled word and in the end Charles lost his patience. He held his glass aloft.

'Come on, I feel like getting rat-arsed. More drinks anyone?'

He was like a chameleon: one moment deadly serious, the next a teenager pushing his boundaries to the limit. Any moment I expected him to suggest we all go to a club, score some coke and do some lines off the taught belly of a lapdancer. What had we let ourselves in for? I swallowed hard and prepared for the worst.

We had been exposed to his eccentric behaviour in the past, a whirling dervish on the dance floor of the Farm Club. The perma-tanned husbands with glistening Rolexes, watching in amusement as he spun their wives round on the dance floor, Charles oblivious to the change in mood and potential confrontation, unable to stop himself before punches were thrown and a hurried exit ensued. There were two personas that inhabited his body and God forbid you should meet Charles in his après-ski world. He said he was only acting up to the crowd, but we knew there was a dark side. We had seen it more than once.

On more than one occasion he had been arrested and locked overnight in a cell. A drunken brawl and a snipe at a policeman outside a Chelsea pub ended with him being thrown head first in to the back of a police van. The police attitude towards drunken behaviour was significantly different back then, but in court Charles always pleaded poverty and usually got away with a small fine.

One night in the middle of summer I was standing next to him outside a Chelsea pub, when the local Sergeant locked eyes on him as he fooled around in the road. Charles liked to intimidate even if the odds were stacked against him.

'Name?'

No reply

'Where do you live?'

'No reply

'Date of birth?'

'30$^{th}$ March'

'Year?'

'Every fucking year.'

'Right. You think you're clever. Throw him in the van.'

I soon realised these were not sporadic incidents. I could be standing in the same space or sitting at the same table and get away scot-free, while Charles was a magnet for heated confrontation and sometimes violence. With John's death still a horrid nightmare, I hoped the dangerous cocktail of painkillers and booze didn't push Charles over the edge. I prayed we didn't see his dark side tonight.

# FIONA'S BEACH PARTY

I sensed Charles had his gun sights firmly fixed on me and I prepared myself for further interrogation.

'So I heard you went to Australia? I'm a little surprised you didn't stay and make a new life for yourself. I can see you struttin' up and down Bondi in tight budgie smugglers.'

I snapped back to the present. 'It's a long story Charles, I'll tell you another time.' I didn't want him to know I had been hauled out of my bed one night and asked in no uncertain terms to leave the country on the next available flight.

'Well don't wait twenty five years.'

I felt like responding with a quip of my own. What were his real reasons for not keeping in touch? But I let it go. I knew he didn't really want to hear about my time spent Down Under. He seemed to have been everywhere except Australia and I knew hearing about the continent's natural wonders and beachside living made him envious.

'Come on, I'm only winding you up.' His voice was childlike, a sardonic whine.

I didn't want to open up more old wounds but I realised I needed to give our leader something to mull over. I released some tension by cracking my knuckles. Charles cringed. It was always the smallest of things that got to him.

'Do you remember Fiona?' I asked.

Monty hummed a familiar tune from the 70's. It was Fiona's song and we sang it whenever we were in her company. She was a mixture of contradictions, fastidious about her appearance, while being obsessed with her prominent nose. It soon became apparent her singular mission in life was to embrace the world that Charles and Monty inhabited and ditch her Aussie roots. Her healthy bank balance made the process easier and almost overnight she began hanging out at ménage-a-trois in Beauchamp Place. Her idols soon became the French chefs Paul Bocuse, Michel Guerard and his pretentious 'Cuisine Minceur.' To the uninitiated it was the healthy, slimming option to fine art on a plate.

'She was the reason I went,' I said.

Charles curled his lip. 'I wonder what happened to her? I bet she went back to Oz to have plastic surgery. She really hated her nose.'

Charles thumped his good hand on the table making other drinkers turn around and stare. 'I heard they modelled Concorde on it.'

Monty gave Charles a long hard stare. Like me, he had always got on well with her. I leaped to her defence. 'Let it go, she had her faults but she had a heart of gold. I stayed with her parents for a few weeks when I was travelling. They lived in Brisbane and had a beach house on the Gold Coast. Her old man was an engineer or something like that and he took me out on his yacht, they were hospitable people with a capital H.'

Monty immediately burst into song. 'I knew an engineer before I died, his wife was never satisfied.'

He had quite a tuneful voice, when he put his mind to it, I thought. Charles attempted to continue with the verse but he stumbled over the rhyming couplets.

'I knew she was fucking loaded. Her overseas fees were monumental and then there was that flat.'

Charles was jealous of anyone with more perceived wealth than him, but I agreed with him, she was properly loaded. Monty broke a short period of contemplation about our old friend. He had been strangely quiet before his recent rugby song outburst.

'She went back to Australia with Simon. You remember him don't you? He rowed for Great Britain.'

I was gob smacked. 'Sorry!'

Monty repeated the sentence.

'Simon, no way!' I replied in disbelief.

'I see a lot of him. He's single now and lives in Clapham. We go out drinking together. Middle-aged bachelors on the town.'

Monty leant forward and held my gaze.

'Oh my God, you don't know!'

I looked at Charles, who raised an eyebrow. He looked as puzzled as I did. Flecks of green sparkled in Monty's eyes; he seemed pleased he had one over on us.

'They got married. It was a complete sham of course. A $15 marriage of convenience to help her stay in the UK.'

I shook my head. 'Simon and Fiona?'

'I told you she was a dark horse,' added Charles.

'It was a secret. They didn't tell anyone until they got back. Simon's parents were furious and refused to acknowledge her as one of the family. The whole episode turned into an horrendous nightmare.'

I was astonished. 'Jesus! Simon and Fiona, married!

'Wait. There's more. Simon's first marriage to Fiona was never annulled. He conveniently forgot about this fairly important fact until he got to the church to take his vows for marriage number two. The wedding had to be hastily adjourned until the legal paperwork had passed through the courts.'

Charles and I were rendered speechless.

The story was even more astonishing because of Simon's upbringing. He was Public School through and through. He had rowed at Henley and the family, who had literary connections, lived in Notting Hill. It didn't get much grander than that. His mother was a fascinating woman, a talented writer and artist, but she was also principled and protective of her boys.

It must have caused quite a stir back in the day, I reflected. I recalled their ostentatious house. 'Do they still live in Notting Hill?' I asked.

'No. His parents sold up years ago and his mother lives in Tuscany now,' Monty explained.

I shook my head. 'How could he possibly forget he was married?'

Charles didn't seem to know anything about this particular mushroom cloud, which surprised me, and it appeared Monty had recovered from his earlier memory lapse, which was promising on all fronts.

'Didn't he go to Radley College?' I asked while I reflected that Public School didn't always go hand in hand with academia.

Charles muttered something scathing under his breath. He never got on with Simon. I think he saw him as a threat to his alpha male status. Monty ignored Charles' sarcasm.

'All three boys went there at various times. It must have cost his parents a fortune. Do you remember going to his house?'

For a brief moment I was briefly transported back to a high-walled courtyard garden on a warm summer's day. Lads in straw boaters, jugs of Pimm's on the lawn, a hammock strung between two fruit laden trees, the air filled with Cuban cigar smoke and John Deacon's drumming.

Charles looked at Monty. 'I remember his mother throwing a tantrum when a neighbour called the police because the music was too loud, but I don't remember his father at all.'

I searched Monty's face for an answer.

'Simon never spoke about his father. It was all really hush-hush. There were rumours he was a spy or on the run from the tax man.'

More Public School secrets I thought.

No-one spoke for a while. I imagined Simon and Fiona on a dusty outback road, the gas pedal of a battered Holden flat to the floor. The newlyweds drinking straight from the bourbon bottle.

Charles broke the extended silence. It was obvious he had been mulling things over in his mind. 'So he'd been banging Fiona on the quiet. The sly old fox.'

Monty had donned half-moon reading glasses and peered down his nose at Charles.

'He obviously didn't need to shout from the rooftops about his bedroom antics like you two.'

Charles loved women. Period. But he had one particular type and that was busty brunettes. I trawled through his list of bed companions and found not one blonde among them. Fiona, ironically, had been blonde and we had all at various times enjoyed her luxurious flat and antipodean hospitality. Even Charles. Her fridge was always stacked with a cornucopia of late-night delicacies: bottles of chilled Chablis, smoked oysters, mussels and bars of white chocolate. There was not a potato scallop or meat pie in sight.

Charles lifted a buttock and farted. I sensed he was still wrestling with the whole Fiona/Simon thing.

'Shagging Fiona would be like shagging your best mate and if you weren't doing it right…' He sneered as his mind grappled for the right words.

Charles whistled through his teeth. 'Pillow talk would have been a fucking ordeal.'

Monty and I exchanged glances. We both knew that if anyone had criticised Charles performances in the sack he would have been mortified. I recalled with fondness the surreptitious nights I spent at Fiona's plush flat, sifting through family albums of her early life on the Gold Coast. There was never any sexual chemistry between us but it was during those purely platonic evenings that she stimulated my interest in travelling overseas, especially to Australia.

Her flat sat directly above La Tante Claire restaurant in Royal Hospital Road. The restaurant was owned by the Roux Brothers and was one of the most expensive and renowned eateries in London, and Charles and Monty were obsessed with its reputation and its Michelin

Stars. At least once a week we would abandon our own flat in favour of Fiona's. Our cab driver seemed perfectly unfazed by our night-time excursions; as if it was perfectly normal for three lads to hail a cab in their dressing gowns, clutching a bottle of gin, Schweppes tonic, ice bucket and breakfast cereal. I cherished those whimsical evenings when we turned up unannounced. The conversations flowed well past dawn and she never once turned us away; they were, in hindsight, the best of times.

'Only a true Aussie could throw a beach party in mid-winter,' I announced.

Charles' eye lit up. It was an evening we would never forget. On the night of the party the pavements in the capital were icy and the roads treacherous; the temperature well below zero. While we waited for someone to let us in, we huddled together, our swimwear hidden beneath heavy coats.

I remembered that I pressed my nose against the frosted glass of the restaurant window and witnessed a mesmerising 'Ballet Gourmande', as dozens of waiters glided between tables of crisp linen, adorned by a sea of crystal. It was like a scene from an old Christmas movie.

Eventually the door buzzed open and we sprinted up the stairs. The scene that confronted us was quite at odds with the fur coats and tiaras seen outside the restaurant. The entire lounge was covered in inches of golden sand and at the far end of the room an Australian flag protruded from an impressive sand castle. Fiona had turned the thermostat up and a mass of bikini clad bodies, gyrated barefoot in a sweltering 30 degrees. Music vibrated though the floor and walls and I wondered how soon it would be before the affluent diners below began to complain to the Maître D' about the noise. Fiona explained later how under intense scrutiny from the restaurant staff below a couple of burly lads from the local builders' merchant had humped the bags of sand up the stairs and deposited it all on plastic sheeting she had laid earlier that day.

The party achieved legendary status. Unfortunately one person didn't want it to end and as chauffeurs arrived to collect the rich and famous from the restaurant below, Charles started a game of volleyball on the pavement.

Charles grinned. 'Come on, lighten up. We weren't hurting anyone. It was just a bit of harmless fun.'

As news spread about the volleyball match, the paparazzi arrived in cars and on scooters and started taking pictures. When someone famous left the restaurant, events soon escalated and began to get out of hand.

Charles had a glint in his good eye. 'If we had played our cards right we could have been on the front of the Daily Mail the next day.'

'Do you mean the list of the fifty most wanted?' Monty fired back.

Charles looked at Monty witheringly. 'I had no idea Thatcher was round the corner holding a cabinet meeting at Chelsea Barracks.'

'So you think standing up to baton-wielding riot police was a good idea.' I said. Charles threw a Nazi salute with his good arm. 'Here's to Thatcher's militia.'

Monty and I hastily scanned the bar to make sure no-one had been offended.

Charles lowered his voice. 'It was only a harmless game of volleyball.'

'You were lucky they didn't lock you up again. I think the fact you were only wearing swimming trunks and sunglasses meant they didn't perceive you as an immediate threat to our Prime Minister.'

'I only asked them if they wanted to play.'

'The police will put those words on your grave,' I said.

Around our table the air was heady with testosterone as we all revelled in the memories of that night; it was like the morning after, when we used to sit around the breakfast table and bait each other with recollections of outlandish actions that we had conveniently erased.

Charles clearly enjoyed a re-run of his fifteen minutes of fame. Nearly thirty years on and it was still his badge of honour: funny, dangerous and downright stupid, it summed the man up perfectly. Unfortunately his appetite for self-destruction was never far from the surface and I watched him knock back two or three glasses in quick succession. If the booze took over I could see a similar outcome tonight; sometimes he was like a child spoiling for a fight. When our laughter subsided Charles seemed in a more reflective mood. Maybe he sensed that I wasn't going to leave this evening without a piece of the truth. I felt more and more that I was in a tense poker game where no-one was sure who had the winning hand. Counter-bluff followed bluff. I was second guessing my motives, I was second guessing everything, so I made a decision and like our troops in the Falklands I decided to go on the offensive. I summoned up all my bravado and unflinchingly, I attempted to wrestle back the initiative. The night was slipping away and I was running out of time.

# JOHN

I caught Charles off guard.

I hadn't meant to confuse him but I could see in his eyes he wasn't sure to which night I was referring. It wasn't a K.O. I had him pinned against the ropes but he recovered well and came out fighting for round two.

'Look, I know I can be a cunt. John died…' He paused '… it's sad, but life goes on.'

I couldn't imagine Charles shedding a single tear. I just couldn't. I sparred with him and tried to hold my nerve. 'Hey, I think we deserve to know the truth, that's all.'

Charles looked at Monty and something passed between them. I can't explain it but at that moment I sensed Monty was in on it.

'He was your twin brother, surely you want to talk about it,' I persisted.

I felt like I was walking the plank, one step away from oblivion. Charles fidgeted; it was as if he was looking for a way out. Then he turned back to me and pursed his lips, a hint of resignation in his demeanour.

'No, you're right.'

At that moment I felt the tide turn. I looked up at the ceiling.

'Just tell us what you're feeling. Jesus, unload for fuck's sake! You'll feel better, I promise you.'

The strain in my voice was all too evident.

'I'd much rather get pissed.' He scratched the skin around his cast. 'A few more glasses and my thumb might stop throbbing.'

I held my breath. I thought for one awful moment he was going to make a U-turn and renege on his promise.

I rambled on. 'Look at us. We are still your mates, or had you forgotten? Don't we deserve to know?'

I caught Monty's expression out of the corner of my eye. I thought he might urge me on but he looked strangely ill at ease.

'We care about you and this has affected you more than you think.'

Charles looked at me, a hint of acceptance in his bloodshot eye. He suddenly aged ten years in as many minutes.

I stood firm. Held his gaze. Charles knew I wasn't about to back down.

'Ok. You win.' He straightened his back and rested

his cast on the table.

He pinched the bridge of his nose with his good hand and closed his eye. He opened it a few seconds later and began talking.

'I presumed John's wife was calling with some news about his work. I asked how bro was; the prolonged silence gave it away. At first she struggled to say anything meaningful although eventually she composed herself long enough to blurt out the terrible news. My twin dead: I wanted to laugh, it seemed absurd. I'm not sure what I felt. Grief does odd things to the mind. I told her not to worry, I would look after her, make everything alright. The clichés kept coming. She pleaded with me not to go, but I needed time to think. I said I would call her right back, but I didn't. I hung up. I walked very calmly to the shed where I kept my emergency pack of ten. Alone in my den I allowed let myself briefly think about mother and father. That's when it dawned on me…I was the only one left: my whole family had been wiped out.'

I smoked one fag down until it burnt my fingers. Somehow I resisted the urge to chain smoke the entire packet. Then I grabbed my car keys and drove to

London. I turned my phone off because I knew his wife would keep calling and it would only hold me up. She had good friends nearby and I knew she wasn't alone, even though her own family lived in Switzerland.

I needed to see John. I took nothing with me and didn't know when or if I would come back. In hindsight, I should have told my wife where I was going, but things are difficult at the moment. I don't remember the drive; it was a blur. I drove fast, I drove angry fast. How I wasn't stopped for speeding I'll never know. I was on auto pilot. One minute I was at home, the next I walked into the mortuary in Wandsworth.'

He paused and wiped his nose with his sleeve.

'It reminded me of an industrial abattoir and that's being kind to the people who design them.'

Charles sniffed the air. 'It smelt of death'.

Monty and I sat quietly and listened. This was the first time we had heard Charles talk this way and we didn't want to interrupt him. The constant chatter in the bar became muted until all we could here was Charles' voice. I sensed he was back with his brother, seeing and feeling it all.

'I phoned Mimi. I assumed friends would be

comforting her, and the children would not have been told anything until we knew for certain, until the body had been identified. Thinking back now, that was what my journey was about. I wanted to be the one to see him first.'

Charles sipped his water. 'She had called her parents, who were flying in from Switzerland the next day. Poor girl she was inconsolable, she kept repeating over and over again. 'It's not true, it's not true. Tell me it's not true Charles.'

A past hamster burial had nearly reduced me to tears and I wondered how anyone dealt with news of that magnitude.

'His wife asked me to identify him.'

Charles took a deep breath as he remembered.

'For a long time I sat outside on a hard plastic chair. I remember thinking: I'm waiting to see my dead brother and you gave me this fucking uncomfortable chair to sit on. I wanted to break the fucking thing, smash it to smithereens. Moments later I was shown into the viewing room. John was lying there peacefully in his rugby shorts. His eyes were closed. His chest had been shaved and there were marks where the crash team had used paddles. Apart from that he was my twin, sleeping. He was still a good looking bastard even in death.'

Monty and I looked down, respectfully avoiding Charles' gaze.

'I remember thinking it was strange that he only had shorts and trainers on. It reminded me of games at school when one team would play in skins. Funny the things you think about when you are taken out of your comfort zone to la-la land.'

At the bar someone clapped and whooped. Charles turned his head, his features full of disgust. I thought he was going to go over and tell them to shut up and show some respect.

He didn't and regained his composure.

'He wouldn't have felt anything. He was dead when he hit the ground. The medics arrived within ten minutes and said they did everything in their power to revive him. At least it was quick: no crippling injuries, no long drawn out terminal illness. I knew I should feel something but I couldn't force a tear out. I was just angry, with everyone and everything.'

'Small comforts,' Monty whispered under his breath.

I sensed Monty wasn't struggling with his emotions

like me.

'Someone must have run to his aid. Someone must have tried to save him.'

With his good hand Charles moved the cruets like pawns on a chess board. 'One minute he was running around, the next…He played every week, on a Tuesday. Christ, he wasn't that old and he was a fit guy. It just goes to show, you never see the grim reaper coming.'

'So what caused it?' I asked.

'The coroner said John had a heart defect in his left ventricle. They told me the Latin term, I just can't remember what it is now. John never knew he had it. Why would he? He'd probably had it since birth. He was just unlucky.'

'First your Dad, now John. Is it congenital?' I asked.

'I know why you are asking. And yes I'm going to get myself checked out as soon as my stitches come out and they give me the all clear.'

'So what happened afterwards?' I asked, wondering how on earth he ended up in Switzerland.

'I went back to John's house. I expected him to open the door and give me a hug. The last time I was there he played me "Your Song" on the piano.'

'He was so proud of his achievement because he hadn't been having lessons for long. He played a few wrong chords but he was good. He just couldn't sing in tune. I sat at his desk and methodically made a list of things to do; find his will, go through all his financial papers, pay any important bills etc, cancel the party. The list went on and on. I decided to use my own lawyer, someone I could trust. Someone I knew would handle the whole thing with dignity and respect.'

'I stayed in London that night and we set the wheels in motion. The following afternoon I flew to Geneva. My last climb of the season. All my kit was abroad so I only needed the basics and I got underwear and toiletries at the airport.'

He held up his plaster cast, as if to say "and then this happened".

'You went skiing! What were you thinking?' I said louder than I meant to.

Charles shrugged his shoulders. 'It was only for a few days. I thought it would clear my head. I didn't want to go home. I needed some time and space to think. One of John's best buddies was a billionaire, a big player in hotels and casinos. I was in contact with him daily until my accident. I signed things off on my Blackberry whenever I needed to.'

'Fucking hell. You could have been on a slab lying next to John. I can't believe any of this. It's totally unreal.'

Charles poked a finger in my direction. I felt his raw anger rise up like a cobra ready to strike.

'Okay don't give me a hard time. What are you, my mother?'

*There's gratitude.*

I never wiped his arse, but saved it on numerous occasions, and why did they both always have to use that turn of phrase? It really grated on me.

Monty excused himself. 'I need to visit the little boys' room.'

I acquiesced. 'Listen. I didn't mean to…I just can't imagine what you must be going through.'

Charles put his good hand on my shoulder. 'Look, I know we all went our separate ways, but I still consider you and Monty to be the only true friends I have. Please though, don't lecture me like I'm still a kid.'

A compliment followed by a reprimand. Typical Charles. I had been put in my place and it hurt, but he was oblivious to my feelings as usual and the mere mention of our enforced parting twisted the knife a little deeper. My eyes misted over, a tear welled in the corner of my eye. I was on the verge of a full-blown tidal wave.

Charles pinched my cheek. 'Leave the tears for the funeral mate.'

Monty returned in the nick of time.

'Hey you two, everything ok?'

I was hurt and for a moment I looked away.

Charles winked at me. It was his way of checking I was ok.

Monty sat down next to me. 'Come on. Let's have a toast to John.'

As Charles stood up I realised we were all hurting in some way or another, it was the supreme irony.

'To John and the "Pimlico Posse", happy times. The best of times.'

I was surprised, because Charles said it all with genuine feeling. Maybe he felt guilty about his earlier outburst.

We raised our glasses, and I caught our reflections in the mirrored ball above the table. Maybe it was a trick of the light but for a fleeting second I saw the three of us fresh-faced, sitting on the wall outside College, unencumbered with the baggage of modern life. However, as I watched us laugh and joke I began to question whether underneath the masks we were the same people?

I first met John on a ski trip to France. It was Easter, near the end of the season, the weather was perfect: factor 10 and t-shirts rather than fleeces. Charles had booked twin rooms in a hosted chalet. We needed an extra person to make the trip affordable so John came. Even after all these years the holiday was still held in some sort of reverence: we should have been blacklisted from ever visiting France again.

We stayed in the old town of Meribel. We were delayed at Grenoble airport and arrived after dinner. It was late and the chalet girls had cleared up and moved on to a bar or a club. The other guests had already retired with the promise of excellent spring skiing conditions the next day. In hindsight we should have joined them. Instead, undeterred by the prospect of an early start the next day, we set off to in search of a local bar. Unfortunately our self-control suffered an early relapse and sometime in the early hours we returned in a boisterous mood to the darkened chalet. In need of a night cap, we discovered the wine store in the basement and unwisely opened a few bottles.

Mayhem soon ensued. Charles and I argued over something trivial and not entirely happy with my point of view Charles grabbed cereal packets from the already laid breakfast table and emptied the contents over my head. I responded by lunging for his arm and ripped his t-shirt; I may even have thrown a punch. There followed an almighty scrum in the kitchen area, which ended in more clothing being ripped and cereal showered everywhere. As if this minor fracas wasn't enough to wake the rest of the chalet's sleeping guests, Monty then proceeded to vacuum up the mess.

Eventually, banging and crashing, we stumbled up to our two rooms in the loft. Monty and John took themselves off, but Charles and I weren't finished. The atmosphere was still sour and edgy and we continued to hurl insults and clothing across the divide between our beds. I couldn't tell you now what we argued over but finally the cat-calling abated and we slept, the matter unresolved but buried until the morning. It was the first and only time we fought and it had as much to do with the cheap French wine as any real malice, but Charles had seen another side to me and I knew it affected him.

The next morning around the breakfast table, uncomfortable silences and conspiratorial whispers followed. Needless to say we were not popular with the other guests, nor the chalet girls after they discovered the empty wine bottles we had hidden under the snow. In the gondola Monty attempted to bring some raison d'être to the night's events but Charles dug his heels in and he never apologised.

John meanwhile watched the first night's debacle with the calm exterior of a conscientious observer. He was a mature, level-headed young man and I'm not sure he knew what to make of it all. I think he was taken aback by his brother's arrogant behaviour and complete lack of self-control. Alas, as the week progressed our conduct only worsened.

We laid siege to this unsuspecting resort like a SWAT team on acid. Our general rowdiness had not gone unnoticed and at the end of one gruelling day I was pinned forcefully to the fence by two Australian ski bums who in no uncertain terms told me to tell my two friends to cool it, otherwise…

'Otherwise what?' Charles said when I told him about my encounter. The following night, undeterred by idle threats, he made a hasty exit through a window of the local bar as he interrupted the evenings rendition of "Tie me kangaroo down sport" with his own verses. Even though we made light of our actions now, looking back I can't say I was proud of our antics. Many were indefensible and downright perilous. Especially the night we redirected all the road signs at the main intersection in the town centre and then watched angry and confused drivers trying to decide which exit to take.

Walking the route home on our last evening, Charles took us up a vertiginous muddy slope. At the top a huge wild boar wallowed in its wooden pen. We had trekked up this same slope a few times before but tonight Charles threatened to release the boar. He was deadly serious and it was only John's stern words that kept the creature in its cage. Thankfully we all made it home in one piece, which is more than can be said for another guest, a pleasant girl from New Zealand. She shattered her tibia midway through the week and subsequently adopted Monty as her crutch for the remainder of the holiday. Kym Thumpkin was her name and Monty looked after her like a small injured bird; his kindness stuck with me because it was a side of him I had never seen before. John sadly never came skiing with us again. I think he'd seen enough of a world he didn't need or want. John was going places and to this day I'm not sure he approved of us.

*John dead.*

I wished I had got to know him better, I wished he'd made it to fifty and seen his children grow up. I only saw him once or twice after that holiday and now he was gone.

I closed my eyes and imagined his lifeless body in the mortuary. Sleeping. That's how I would come to terms with a tragedy of that magnitude. I would pretend he was sleeping. Of course that was nonsense; he wasn't a furry animal, he was a miracle of evolution. I wasn't religious but I wondered where his spirit was right now. Maybe it was right here in the room hovering above us and Charles didn't know. I shook the image of John's lifeless body from my mind, it was upsetting me again.

Charles poured himself more wine.

'What happened to him after University?' I persisted.

'He was headhunted by Unilever and ended up as

CEO of an advertising agency. Don't ask me how he got there. I don't think John knew himself. He always had a knack of falling on his feet. He always knew the right people, was always in the right place at the right time.'

'You said he'd been under a lot of stress,' I said.

'Let's say he ran into a few problems.'

'Like?'

'There was going to be a company takeover. John had the support of some of the Board, but it was stab-you-in-the-back time and he had two kids at private school, a massive mortgage to service and more to lose than anyone else.'

'Bastards.'

'My motto is trust no–one, but unfortunately John trusted everyone.'

'He'd been pretty successful then?' I asked.

'You could say that. It was nothing like Branson and Virgin but it was high-powered shit all the same. To his credit he never bigged himself up, kept his feet firmly on the ground and was highly respected within the industry. He used to manage one of the formula one accounts and was always jetting off to Monaco or Verbier for the weekend. When things were going well he got himself a share in a restaurant in Chelsea and a big fat Harley. Then everything changed. A whistleblower uncovered the coup d'état, but when John realised the Board were about to shaft him it was too late. He felt betrayed: he had built the company up from nothing. He took it personally and although he never admitted it, he became very depressed. To keep him buoyant he occasionally relied on coke and amphetamines.'

'He rang me a few weeks ago to say he was putting together a plan with a venture capital firm to buy back part of the business. He sounded more upbeat and we started discussing a joint party. He told me he was happy to organise it, he had a great venue in mind and would confirm all the details soon. I could tell he was excited about it. That was the last time I spoke to him.'

'Shit Charles. I am so, so sorry, 'I said.

'Yeah, I can't say I feel like celebrating this birthday.'

The words made him sound like a man without friends, which he certainly was not, although I sensed he was not telling me the whole story about his life in Shropshire.

## TWINS

Charles married his College sweetheart. The wedding took place in the autumn of 1984, the year of Live Aid. I wasn't aware that Charles had got Mel pregnant, which made me deliberate about the reason for such a hastily arranged wedding only a few months after finishing College.

Monty told me it was a lavish affair. The bride and bridesmaids were dressed in swirls of matching cream, Mel ferried to church in an open top horse and carriage, while the rest of the entourage were driven in white Mercedes' festooned with garlands. Many of their friends from London made the journey up the M6; however, when I heard Monty had been best man, some sixth sense told me something didn't add up. As Charles filled in the gaps I mulled over the facts. John was an usher. Surely John would have been best man to his brother's wedding?

Perhaps John and Charles had fallen out or maybe John wasn't up to the task, maybe he was ill, maybe he had lost his voice? I certainly wouldn't have enjoyed that level of responsibility and for reasons unknown to me I had never been asked to be best man for any of my friends. Maybe I wasn't reliable. Maybe I wasn't a safe choice.

*Once an usher, always an usher.*

In the end I let it go. I couldn't see it had anything to do with our last night in London all those years ago. And, if I was honest, apart from an unquenchable desire to see how our lives had unravelled, that was the main reason I showed up tonight.

Their wedding took place in a picturesque village near Shrewsbury and was followed by a reception at the family home, a grand mock Tudor mansion about ten miles outside Chester. It appeared I had missed quite an event in the social calendar. Monty believed it had made the newlyweds pages in Tatler.

I studied Charles as he trawled through his version of events and long before I found out that the Caribbean island of St Kitts was the destination for the honeymoon I sensed something untoward had happened that day. It was Monty who let the cat out of the bag and no amount of pleading from Charles could stop him.

The bride and groom spent their first night of wedded bliss at the Grosvenor Hotel in Chester. Around the time they began their journey to the hotel, Monty, John and Simon left the reception and drove at break neck speed to the town centre.

Monty shook his head. 'No-one should have driven anywhere, we were all well over the limit.'

The plan, and Monty explained it was a very loose plan at that stage, was to get to the hotel before them and ambush them. While Charles did his best to interrupt Monty's flow, I sat riveted, but already feared a catastrophe in the making. With a little help from a few gullible hotel staff, John and Monty manned the reception desk, while remarkably Simon was given access to the bridal suite and amused himself with miniatures from the well-stocked mini bar.

The stage was set and all three waited on tenterhooks for the bride and groom to arrive. When they arrived in the foyer, Monty greeted them and acted as concierge, carrying their bags to the suite. Meanwhile John alerted Simon by phone that they were on their way up. Charles thought it was all entertaining stuff and played along, the perfect stooge. It was all good natured and humorous up to this point.

The happy couple presumed the prank ended with

Monty doffing his top hat for a tip at their door; they had no idea Simon, having consumed most of the mini bar, was hiding under the bed.

Simon decided to wait a few minutes and then roll out and give them a fright. However, the longer he remained under the bed the more difficult it became to choose the right moment to exit. If, of course, there is a right time for attempting something that stupid. This was Charles on his wedding night.

John and Monty sat at the bar and waited for Simon to appear downstairs in the lobby. After a while they feared something had gone horribly wrong.

Meanwhile up in the bridal suite Simon remained under the bed while the bride and groom chatted. In the fullness of time, baths were run, dressing gowns were donned, champagne was opened, lights were dimmed, and…

For nearly an hour Simon lay corpse like under the bed and it was only when it became evident the happy couple were about to conjugate their marital rights, right above his head, that Simon bit the bullet and rolled out.

Monty was only able to paint a sketchy picture of what happened next and with some reticence allowed

Charles to finish the story. Mel screamed and ran naked to the safety of the bathroom. Simon ran for the door. Charles, like a gunfighter, stood his ground, dressing gown open, his impressive erection visible, leaving Simon in no doubt that he was in the mood. Whatever Charles could lay his hands on followed Simon to the bedroom door: shoes, ice bucket, fruit and an expensive vase, which was put on their bill when they left.

Simon escaped with his life and the conspirators drove back to the reception and partied until dawn. Afterwards Monty, John and Simon were all summoned to apologise to Mel. Monty and John were forgiven; however, Simon bore the brunt of Charles temper and the two didn't speak for some considerable time afterwards.

A twisted part of me wished I had been there under the bed with Simon, I wished I had seen the shock on Charles' face, but while friendships were being sorely tested back in the UK, I was starting a new life on other side of the world. Ever since Skippy hopped across our black and white TV screens and Jacques Cousteau's 'Calypso' brought the Barrier Reef into our dreary suburban living rooms, I dreamt of eating Vegemite sandwiches on white beaches where the sun shone all day. Simple, uncomplicated sun-drenched pleasures. Underneath of course I was running away from all the shit. My parents had just divorced and I had no desire to return to the UK for a very, very long time.

I should have been able to shut Charles and Monty out of my thoughts, as I sampled the delights of tropical North Queensland and the Barrier Reef, but that July night still gnawed away at me, their youthful faces never completely forgotten. My mother, bless her, kept me in touch with important events back home. She was a keen letter-writer and with international telephone calls difficult to organise when you were on the move on the other side of the world she began to use the medium of tape messages to great effect.

Unaware I had left the country to work in Australia, Charles sent my wedding invitation to my parents' house. When I received the news from my mother I was surprised by my conflict of emotions. I was initially surprised, then suspicious, then angry and finally dismissive. I had moved on from my old life in England, I didn't need them anymore. However over the following days and weeks events back in the UK niggled away at me and soon I began to feel different. Maybe in part it was due to my girlfriend of the time running off with a water-skiing instructor.

I feared I might have got it all horribly wrong: These were not the actions of a person who wanted to cut off all contact and I was concerned I had developed a sense of paranoia about certain aspects of our relationship and their disappearance that night. Surely those indiscretions were all part of growing up and perhaps there had been a perfectly rational explanation all along. As usual I overthought it. Was I going to waste my entire life going over and over the same ground? No. I was living the dream and my life had moved on, I was too far away to be chased by shadows.

Tonight, in the cosseted intimacy of our corner booth it appeared our youthful spirits were still alive and kicking and for a while I completely forgot my true reason for being here. Charles was in good form, his moral compass askew once more. After he finished his wedding story we trawled through our ribald past. These flights of fancy ranged from Charles and I undertaking interior decorating while on hallucinogenic drugs and three-legged beer races round the pubs of Kensington and Chelsea. I recalled Charles and Mel in the early days and how, right from the start, they endured a love-hate relationship.

Charles in his own inimitable style had done everything within his power to wind Mel up, which wasn't difficult because Mel took after her mother: she was far too trusting and once Charles caught the scent of weakness he was like a dog with a bone, he wouldn't let it go. To be fair the contest was not completely one-way traffic and Mel gave as good as she got, but never an argument went by when we didn't think that, underneath all the bitching and backstabbing, there was serious sexual chemistry at work.

I discovered that after the wedding Charles moved out of London to rural Shropshire, where he had lived ever since. Here his business empire had flourished and he proceeded to list the assets he had accrued over the years: rental properties, shares, cars, wine, art, you name it he seemed to have it all.

'You know me, I can't read or write but set me a task with my hands and...'

I cut in to his dialogue. It was a risky move, but I felt he had chilled sufficiently after the burden of John's death had been lifted from his shoulders.

'Monty said you'd turned your hand to property developing.'

I knew Charles could fix a bike or car with his eyes shut and I suppose building construction was just the next logical step.

'Where did you learn how to do that?' I asked, instantly regretting asking a dumb question that I already knew the answer to.

Charles face was full of disdain. He didn't need to reply, his look said it all. If builders can do it, so can I.

I made a rash attempt at extricating myself from the very large hole I was rapidly disappearing into. 'Look this might be old news to you, but when God was dishing out the engineering genes I missed out. I can't even put a shelf up straight,' I said.

Charles held up his good hand. Like Monty's it dwarfed mine. 'These hands could tell some stories.'

I sensed Charles was about to launch once again into his favourite subject and neatly diverted his thoughts. I knew enough about his past sex life to keep me entertained for the rest of the evening and beyond.

'Do you have any more projects on the horizon?' I spluttered, my wine finding the wrong way down.

Charles was thrown for a second as he decided which line of thought to pursue. Lurid sex stories or elucidating on his building acumen. I was amazed the buildings won.

'At the moment I'm in the middle of constructing a timber cabin. It's on the edge of the woods backing on to the yard at work. It's not your bog-standard mobile home, this is a high end studio with all mod cons.'

Charles nudged me with his good arm. 'My private space, where I can escape from the world. And my wife. It will have to wait to be finished now. I can't work a nail gun one-handed.'

Charles pondered for a moment.

Monty kicked him under the table, knowing that's exactly what Charles was thinking of doing.

Charles shuffled out of range of Monty's brogue and excused himself. I wasn't one to gloat but I sensed Charles was papering over the cracks and I sensed more than a hint of a marriage in turmoil. While Charles was in the cloakroom, I thought about Mel. A lifetime under the same roof: She needed a medal for valour. Charles returned and sat down heavily next to me. A roll of flesh hung over his belt; he had put on weight.

'You've been married nearly as long as…' I stopped

myself; we all knew the significance of the gap. 'I don't know how Mel has put up with you, I really don't.'

I was half-joking but knew I could get away with it. Charles would agree whole-heartedly that he was the most difficult person to live with. Monty and I were excluded from this of course because somehow, many years ago, we had managed to earn his respect. Don't ask me how or why. It was as David Attenborough put so succinctly 'one of life's great mysteries.'

'We've had our ups and downs, like everyone,' Charles continued.

'It was Mel who wanted kids, I don't have a paternal bone in my body. I always needed a separate life away from my family.'

I felt the green shoots of envy take hold again, I knew I didn't want his life but I couldn't help myself wanting all the five star trappings.

'Of course family holidays are different, you are away from home and everyone is more relaxed but at home, day-to-day living, I don't enjoy that whole family unit thing.' I had to pinch myself because Charles appeared to be in full off-loading mode.

'How many kids do you have?' I asked.

'Three. Jamie is the eldest and I have two girls. My son is already taller than me and drinks like a fish.'

Just like his father I thought, as I recalled a rugby tour to Plymouth where Charles collapsed after a drinking game involving a huge chess board where pints of bitter replaced the regular chess pieces.

'He wants to be a doctor. Why not set your standards high? I'm not sure I ever did.'

I gazed at the gleaming Rolex watch on his wrist. It was a strange comment to make because it was evident Charles had done very nicely for himself.

'The girls idolise Mel. The three of them spend most of their time together: shopping, restaurants, holidays; high maintenance would be an understatement.'

Mel and her sister had both been excessively spoilt by their father, a self-made millionaire who doted on his daughters to the point of suffocation. His business interests had morphed into various separate companies that evidently had all become successful in their own right.

I thought Charles may have been a little more magnanimous as I reflected his sole objective right from the start might have been to take over one of the more high-profile companies. It left me to speculate about Charles' real motives. I wasn't sure if Charles' back story was for my ears only, because if Monty knew more, he wasn't saying. He was currently in an intimate conversation with someone on the next table. I got the impression the two knew each other. Maybe he was an old school friend. I sat back and let Charles illuminate me further.

'Mel took John's death worse than I did. It was suffering and grief beyond her comprehension. She couldn't imagine how she would cope if her sister was gone. It sounds ghoulish but none of us would have been sad if it had been her father. Not even Mel. He was a self-made man, a real control freak and constantly tried to drive a stake between us, which just pushed Mel further away from him.'

Another selfish man I thought, no wonder they never got on.

I subconsciously glanced at my watch. It was 10pm. Time was moving quickly. My stomach grumbled and I wondered when last orders were. I hadn't eaten since breakfast. Charles fidgeted in his seat, he was obviously in considerable discomfort and I wondered if he might leave here in an ambulance rather than a taxi.

'Mel and Tash are still joined at the hip; we go to balls together and the occasional meal in town and every May I take all the girls for a week's holiday in Cyprus. Sometimes I feel like I am married to both of them.'

The next words slipped out. I couldn't help myself. 'Did you ever...?'

Charles finished my sentence. '...think about sleeping with Tash? We came close a few times when we were drunk but sorry to spoil your fantasy, it never happened. She is more like a sister.

'Did she get married?' I asked.

'Yes. Eventually she settled down and found "Mr Right". She married a local lad in the same church we got married in. Oh, and how about this for a coincidence. His family owned a chain of delicatessens and guess where the original one was?'

I hated guessing games. I tried to look like I was giving the question some serious thought, while instead I was remembering a sweet shop I had visited as a nipper in the 1970s. It was the kind that had all the sweets in jars and your selections were weighed and dispensed in small paper bags. I closed my eyes and I could smell the sickly scent of pear drops. However while we were at College I discovered the chain of shops had been co-incidentally owned by Charles' late mother. It was indeed a small world.

'In bloody Pimlico,' Charles announced loudly.

'You're kidding. I remember the pubs, corner shops, and cafes but I don't

remember any posh delis.'

'I don't know when it opened its doors; however it was one of the first to bring in all the luxury brands, the best truffles, oils and charcuterie that Italy had to offer. Maybe they opened it after we left London.'

*Truffles.*

A wry smile played on my lips at the mention of truffles.

Charles and truffles; he had been an authority on the subject. He knew where to search for them, which pigs and dogs had the required finely tuned sense of smell to find them and the best ways to serve them. I think the real reason that he liked to talk about truffles was because they were hard to find and expensive; like gulls' eggs, or shark fin soup, it was a supply and demand equation and Charles loved anything exclusive. I didn't understand what all the fuss was about; they were simply overpriced, slightly perfumed, mouldy tubers.

Charles embraced gastronomy like a duck to water and became obsessed by anything that was edible, exotic and unusual. His tastes were all-encompassing and for a while he had an unhealthy fascination with sea urchins, something he had eaten in the Galapagos Islands, where he had travelled after leaving school. I recalled how he forced everyone to listen to his tales about hitching rides aboard merchant vessels and his near fatal battle with dysentery, and if he felt you weren't utterly convinced by his 'Hemingway' spirit he would produce his annotated albums that mapped out his entire six month passage to far flung places.

Charles turned my face to the side so he could study my profile.

'Come to think of it Tash's husband looked very similar to you. He was short and dark, not bad looking, just like you when you had more hair. I wonder what Tash saw in vertically challenged men?'

'We're just better in bed,' I smirked.

'Yeh and I've got a small dick…anyway, it's ironic in a way because Tash desperately wanted children but she suffered miscarriage after miscarriage. Poor girl, she went to see a specialist about a medical condition whose name I can't remember. They advised her that surgery was her best option. Sadly it failed. After that their options were limited. They considered surrogacy for a while but in the end, because they had left it too late, adoption was the only option.'

As Charles talked, I reflected that there were a whole host of people from my past I hadn't thought about in a long time and apart from the recent medical diagnoses, which struck a bitter chord, I was enjoying the sentimental journey. However I needed to focus on the present and there and then I made a pact with myself: I vowed to improve on my life skills and try and rekindle my lost mojo before it was too late. I turned to face my tormentor, my veins full of renewed possibilities.

'They adopted two boys.' Charles beamed, showing me a perfect set of expensive white teeth.

I hesitated. 'Not...'

'Yup, twin boys. Angelic faces, but underneath real monsters. Tash is not the best disciplinarian in the world.'

I rubbed the stubble on my chin. 'What is it with your

family and twins?'

Mel and Tash were also non-identical twins.

'Don't ask me. I'm just relieved the genes didn't continue for us. Then again, genetic conditions are quite random, it can skip entire generations.'

Charles was still a sponge when it came to absorbing facts.

'It's all to do with the gene pools. Twin births involve a unique set of circumstances and are not hereditary, as everyone thinks. I just wish Tash didn't dress the boys the same. They look like Tweedle Dum and Tweedle Dee. Thank God my mother never did that to me and John. In fact it was quite the opposite, most people never knew we were even brothers.'

I had to agree with him. I would have had a DNA test, I thought.

I looked across at Monty and I knew we were both itching to ask the same question; however, I thought long and hard about how Charles would react before I launched in.

'Did you feel or sense anything the night John died?'

A recent documentary I had seen on TV researched personality traits, mannerisms and attitudes of dozens of pairs of twins. Many of the twins shared these common qualities and a few experienced similar thought patterns, a sense of déja vu and feeling the pain of another. I found the findings intriguing but they were inconclusive, a bit like the studies undertaken to investigate eidetic and photographic memory, which I had more than a passing interest in.

Charles considered the question for longer than I expected.

'Before all of this happened I may have dismissed it all as tosh, but...'

Monty and I leant forward expectantly.

'So did you?' I pressed.

Charles' face softened.

'I had been sifting through a stack of old family photographs. I was organising them into some sort of order. There were a few holiday snaps of John looking far too cool in his Ray Bans. Then, wedged at the bottom, I came across a picture almost torn in half. It was of John sitting at the piano.'

I looked across at Monty. Goose bumps ran up my arms.

'The photograph was ruined so I screwed it up and

binned it. I vaguely remember the phone call from his wife came shortly afterwards. I didn't feel a stabbing chest pain if that's what you mean.'

I turned to Monty. 'Co-incidence?'

Monty shrugged his shoulders. Maybe, maybe it was some sort of... '

Charles sighed.

'Well whatever theory you choose to make of it is fine by me, because he's gone and nothing can bring him back. John loved that piano. He couldn't sing for toffee, but he wasn't bad at thumping out a tune.'

Charles steeled himself. He wasn't going to let emotion play any part in this evening.

'If Mimi is forced to sell John's house and downsize, what will she do with a white Steinway? It's not an ornament, it needs to be played.'

Charles looked up to the heavens. I expected him to shake his good fist at an unrighteous God. Instead he spat the words out.

'It's all so shitty for them.'

Charles excused himself and went to stretch his legs, although it wouldn't have surprised me if he had gone in search of the flirtatious waitress. Monty and I were silent for a while. I pursed my lips and let out a long breath, like I was blowing pollen from a dandelion.

'Thanks for not mentioning the book. I couldn't go through a long-winded explanation with him at the moment. He is not in the right place to understand the lives of mere mortals.'

The daily grind of survival that he clearly knows nothing about, I thought.

Monty smiled.

'It will be our secret, just keep me up to speed on its progress because I want to be there to celebrate if you write a bestseller. I want to walk next to you on the red carpet.'

I sensed it was time to lighten the tone. I wanted to find out more about his time in Asia. Monty had visited Ho Chi Minh City, the old Saigon, and he recalled the Vietnamese as friendly and the city as cosmopolitan, overflowing with bicycles and scooters. He had been lucky enough to be invited to lavish banquets and when he described the vibrant street markets and the delicate, exotic Asian flavours, it made me want to get on the next plane.

He visited the Vietcong tunnels but he was

disappointed that many of the other war relics were sadly now commercial tourist traps. The grandeur of the hotels and the French influence in architecture was a million miles from the images I had seen of rice fields and waterways crammed with outriggers steered by women wearing lampshade hats.

'And the women?' I pressed.

Monty winked. 'No doubt you would enjoy them. They are very attentive.'

'Tell us more about the one that got away. What was she like?'

Monty's eyebrows furrowed. 'I worked with her in Vietnam. She was Cambodian by birth and worked as a translator for a hotel chain. She was like a fragile china doll. You both would have approved.'

I conjured up an image of a geisha girl with a tiny waist and jet black hair; a strange pairing, if I was perfectly honest.

'But when the time came to plan our future together, I bottled it and bolted like a thoroughbred horse leaving the stalls. Well that was that. I resumed my camaraderie with the Head Chef and on our days off we returned to the flesh pots of the nearest city.'

I had been to Thailand on my honeymoon and it was easy to imagine Monty walking the steamy back streets, air thick with the pungent aromas of street food, windows lit by phosphorescent neon signs, while bikini clad girls posed for onlookers in the windows. Many with their creamy skin, long legs and chiseled features seemingly far too perfect.

Monty was oblivious to my reverie.

'You know my problem. I can't commit. I never liked feeling tied down, the pressure, the expectation, it was all too much.'

Charles returned and leered at a passing waitress, who hurried past his outstretched plaster cast. He caught the end of our conversation. 'I don't mind being tied down, the tighter the better.'

We both tried to ignore him, but it was difficult. He was a force to be reckoned with even when he was suffering.

'Don't you ever get lonely?' I asked Monty again.

Charles carefully squeezed himself back into the booth.

'You never gets lonely do you Monts? He loves his books and his food and he has his extended family in

Sweden to keep him busy.' Charles tapped his nose with a finger. 'He has discerning tastes now. He likes the oriental look.'

*Why was Charles coming to Monty's rescue?*

Monty raised his eyebrows at me. It was obvious he didn't appreciate Charles talking for him.

Almost at the same time I felt Charles hone in like a heat-seeking missile. The booze was turning him again and the atmosphere altered once more.

'So, are you shagging out of the marital bed?'

The question was so random and unexpected I felt like I had been slapped.

'Fuck off Charles. What sort of question is that? It's none of your business,' I said vehemently.

'I heard you married a nice looking Swede.'

My wife wasn't Swedish. Her first name was derived from the Germanic. Her father had done his national service in the mountains of Austria and named his only daughter after an Austrian princess.

'You know I have a sneaking suspicion that Monty and I were once acquainted with your lovely wife.'

I experienced a sinking feeling in my stomach. 'And how's that?' I said, feeling the world tilt a little further.

*My wife!*

'Well Monty will remember this. The year after my wedding I organised a ski trip.'

Charles was always happiest talking about the mountains and he seemed to get a second wind. He pointed at Monty with his good hand.

'You spent ten hours in the toilets at the Farm Club.'

I was relieved Charles had turned his attention away from me and waited for Monty to elaborate on his escapade. I secretly hoped Charles was just trying to wind me up.

I watched Monty construct the story in his mind before he spoke.

'The weather was atrocious, fog like pea soup and it was snowing heavily. By lunchtime I had had more than enough. The visibility on the slopes was down to a few yards. I left my skis at the Medran lift and walked down the hill into the village. Maybe it was a dodgy oyster from the night before but I suddenly needed a crap really badly. In a blind panic I knocked on the door of the Farm Club. I squatted against the wall and waited for what seemed an eternity until I heard the door being unlocked. A cleaner opened the door. I think she was expecting a delivery but when she saw the look of desperation on my face, she took pity on me and ushered me in. I was so relieved I could have kissed her.'

I butted in. 'So you went into the cloakroom, took a crap and what? Fell asleep?'

Monty snorted.

'I went out like a light. I was knackered; we hadn't slept in days. It was afternoon so the Club was empty and I slept through til the evening. The next thing I heard was music and someone taking a piss in the next cubicle. The dozy cleaner must have presumed I'd let myself out and had gone home. I tried to sneak out, but I was seen by one of ski guides who wanted to buy me a drink. I saw no point in going back to the chalet so I went back to the bar. I still had my boots and goggles on.'

Monty pointed at Charles. 'When this lot turned up later all suited and booted, they presumed I had just started early.'

Charles gestured with his good hand. 'Little did we know.'

I was so wrapped up in the story that I was caught completely off guard when Charles resumed his story about my wife. It appeared my execution had merely been postponed.

'We met this girl, she worked as a nanny.'

My world spun. 'You must be mistaken.'

Charles tapped his nose with the index finger of his good hand.

'Everyone has a past.'

I became defensive. 'You're making this up!'

'It's the truth.' Disturbingly, Monty nodded in agreement.

'Ha ha, very funny.' I pretended to laugh. I wasn't very convincing.

Charles punched my shoulder. 'When you get home you should ask her.'

Charles loved to think he had something over you. It was his way of exerting control. I felt angry and confused. Why wouldn't my wife have told me she knew them?

'Why don't you believe me?' Charles asked.

'Because I don't.'

'Look do you remember Niki from St George's Square? Her sister worked for Supertravel. They were all there: Sarah, Kerry, they spent the whole season together.'

I shook my head.

Charles shrugged his good shoulder. 'It's a small world isn't it?'

I didn't know whether to believe him or not. It was too much to take in and I felt bewildered. The whole thing was farcical. The only option was to ask my wife, but I wasn't sure it was a question I wanted to know the answer to.

Please God, don't let her be involved in any of this.

Charles sensed he had pushed too far and he backed off a little, maybe remembering our scuffle in the chalet.

'You've got two kids then, a boy and a girl.'

*He knew everything. Always had, always would.*

My mouth felt dry and I swallowed hard. 'Fifteen and seventeen now,' I replied proudly.

Charles smirked like a Cheshire cat. 'Monty told me you used to live in Kingston, near Richmond Park.'

It was a difficult period in my life. We had just purchased a flat, interest rates rocketed, money was tight and we struggled to conceive. It was an incredibly stressful time. I didn't really want to discuss my inner turmoil with him but there were similarities to Tash's troubles that I wanted to air.

I wanted him to know not everyone's life had been plain sailing.

'We also had problems conceiving, the specialist initially thought it was my wife but they discovered the problem was a little closer to home.'

I regretted saying the words as soon as they left my mouth. Charles didn't need any more information. He got it in one.

'Oh my God! You of all people!'

My stomach churned. I didn't want Charles to wade in any further, so I thought I would make light of my predicament and turn it into an anecdote. Even in the comfort of a busy bar I felt alone and vulnerable again, like I was dropping my trousers for the doctor and nurses at the fertility clinic.

'I had to deliver my samples to a clinic at Kingston Hospital. I have never felt so embarrassed and each time I crept along the corridor and hurriedly left my sample on the hatch before anyone saw me.'

Charles nudged Monty. 'Who would have thought it? Ben firing blanks.'

'It's not much fun, I can vouch for that. Have you ever tried jacking off into a test tube?'

Charles was tempted to laugh but stopped. The thought of his virility being questioned was akin to a world that had stopped turning on its axis. Momentarily it stopped him in his tracks. I reflected how the wine and drugs were making him more and more unpredictable. Charles had a short fuse and this made him all the more volatile. Monty was clearly oblivious to any impending disaster and was busy checking messages on his ancient Nokia phone.

Charles leaned over coyly and stroked my arm. One minute aggressive, the next sweetness personified. It really kept you on your toes.

'You know Tash still has a soft spot for you.'

It was a lifetime ago but I still blushed. I couldn't help it.

I knew exactly where Charles was going with this; it was an evening I hadn't thought about in a long time.

Mel's sister moved to London and enrolled on a beauty course at the London School of Fashion. The twins shared a flat near Gloucester Road and they invited Charles and I for dinner. Monty was otherwise engaged with an old friend from Wrekin, and anyway, three would have been a crowd. Right from the start the warning signals were there.

Charles decided we should make an effort and after much deliberation we decided to go in black tie. He drove us there in his yellow Mini, a car that had only recently survived an altercation with a half-built roundabout near the much-hyped new ring road, the M25. Charles came in much too fast, hit the kerb and flew like a missile into the middle of it. I thought we were all dead. We were lucky and the Mini got away with buckled tracking rods.

'Well the least said about that the better,' said Charles.

He was immensely proud of his driving skills, in much the same way his was proud of his skiing and performances in the sack. Tonight I discovered he had twice taken part in the RAC rally, long before he got bitten by the extreme mountain sports bug. Needless to say, he always drove too fast, right on the edge. On one occasion he apparently left a wedding to get a pack of cigarettes (he was high as a kite) and cornered too fast on a country road. He was in a kilt and had to phone Mel to get someone to come and release him. When his friends arrived they found him still strapped in, hanging upside down, with his tackle swinging in the breeze.

The girls' flat was in Draycott Mansions, an impressive building, opulent and palatial. It had an intercom entry phone system and the foyer smelt of beeswax. The corridors were a sea of lush blue carpet, monogrammed in gold; all that was missing was a doorman in a top hat and long coat. It was the complete antithesis of our stuffy flat in Pimlico.

The flat was owned by their father. He allowed the girls to use it as a base while they were studying in London, but they had to be constantly on their guard because they never knew when he might just pop in unannounced. I remembered he had parochial views when it came to the touchy subject of sex before marriage, which ironically was very similar to my own experiences with the Irish Catholic family I was to marry into.

We were ushered into an open plan dining and living area, seductively lit by candlelight. The table was laid with the best crystal glasses and a decanter of red wine. I was unable to remember what we ate that evening and decided it probably hadn't been that memorable; besides, it soon became evident the girls had more important things on their minds.

Monty looked up from his phone. 'Mel was possibly the worst cook I've ever met.'

After all these years, Charles still loved to put her down.

'She still is. She told me she was cooking lamb the other day. When she took it out of the oven it had miraculously turned itself into an over-cooked rib of beef. Needless to say, when I'm at home I do all the cooking.'

After dinner, the girls suggested we adjourn to the sofa for coffee. Charles thought about ordering a cab because he was too pissed to drive. I have no idea why we were trying to escape; maybe it was a sixth sense telling us to get the hell out of there before anything we might regret later occurred. In hindsight, we didn't need much persuading to stay.

The lights dimmed and we all made ourselves comfortable on a splendid red sofa. Within seconds and at the push of a button the sofa turned into a double bed, and very soon all four us were writhing about half-clothed. Before the foreplay got out of hand we were dragged off to separate bedrooms and Charles was introduced properly to his future wife.

Charles gesticulated rudely with his good arm.

'I thought it was a free for all at that point.'

This little interlude obviously brought back good memories for Charles and he banged his good arm on the table a few times. A couple trying to have an intimate evening turned and stared at him again.

'Still the loudest table,' Monty announced.

'The next morning, I stumbled into the bathroom and found Charles in the bath, washing his tackle. I sat on the toilet and we chatted. His back was covered in scratches, bright red welts. To this day I have never seen such a crime of passion.'

Charles preened like a peacock.

'Badge of honour mate. Mel's nails were like razors. I think she filed them down that night especially for me.'

My night of passion with Mel's sister was a one-off, although for Charles it was just the beginning and he began to spend more time at Draycott Mansions, tempted by clean sheets, duck-down pillows and a long soak in a bubble bath. For Monty and I, our occasional meal of sausage, cabbage and mash became a meal pour nous deux.

His occasional absences created a little more space and the flat was less messy but there was something missing. A void. Our ship had lost its captain. We realised we missed his outrageous, bawdy behaviour. We missed his intractable resolve, his unwavering confidence, his forthright opinions. We missed his protective arm, his passions, even his bloody tantrums. We wanted him back.

## BOEUF BOURGUIGNON

We didn't have long to wait.

Charles' tempestuous relationship with Mel continued throughout College, brief periods of lust were interspersed with prolonged periods of singledom. The courtship followed a familiar pattern: he would leave Mel at least once a week and turn up on our doorstep without his front door key. While we kept him standing in the cold he would announce to the whole street that she was a "fucking bitch and it was over.' Which it was, until he needed a shag and back he went between Mel's thighs.

With or without him, Monty and I divided our time between Winchester Street and 64 St George's Square, a smart second floor flat occupied by three girls from the Home Counties who were training to be cordon bleu chefs. I was told their fathers did something important in the city, something that afforded the blonde one's parents a pied-à-terre just round the corner.

Like Charles and Monty they had been educated at Private School and all had ponies and pools in the grounds. I knew little about pony club and dressage, subjects on which they could talk for hours; however, living in London had caused them to undergo a frantic transformation, that meant they now smoked Marlboro reds, swore like troopers and cycled everywhere (because it was cheaper than taxis) on old fashioned bicycles with wicker baskets. They were as close to real Sloanes as you could get, right down to their headscarves, pearls and scuffed, tasselled loafers. There was not a jodhpur in sight.

They worked as chalet girls in the winter and spent summers serving champagne and canapés aboard luxurious yachts in the South of France. It was no surprise therefore that they were more than happy to show off their cooking skills to two or three good-looking hungry lads. Their flat was on the other side of Pimlico in a tranquil leafy haven, a stone's throw from the embankment. During the summer, the tree-lined square attracted an eclectic mix of sun worshipers, yoga classes and book worms, while on exceptionally hot days the girls took us, via a concealed stairwell, onto the flat roof where they could secretly sunbath topless.

It wasn't that we disliked our flat; far from it, it hosted many memorable parties where a bounty of illicit substances were cut, smoked and inhaled. However, being predominately underground meant it felt claustrophobic and for much of the year the rear garden hardly caught the sun. This minor oversight on my behalf meant that if the temperature soared our only option was to take some rather expensive sofa cushions up onto the street and sunbathe on the pavement. Charles took an armchair up once and caused quite a stir amongst the local residents, who left a note on our railing explaining that we were lowering the tone of *their* street. This wasn't Ladbroke Grove they pointed out in large red letters.

The roof top of St George's Square afforded unrestricted views across London, to the City in the East and across the river to Battersea Power Station. The northern end of the square was buttressed by the largest self-contained block of flats in Western Europe. Dolphin Square, built in 1935, epitomised stylish living and would have made a perfect back-drop for a John Le Carré spy novel. Over the years, with its grand reception hall, restaurant and bar, shops and indoor swimming pool, it gained notoriety: a home to Lords, politicians and celebrities alike. Christine Keeler lived there for a short time and John Vassall, the Soviet spy, was arrested at his apartment in 1962. I knew no-one that renowned or glamorous, although a College friend named Bubbles stayed there occasionally when his father was away overseas with the military.

Bubbles was a flamboyant dresser and not averse to wearing eyeliner, which along with his penchant for leather trousers gave him a decidedly camp look. Sadly he lost a friend in the Falklands war and left College having lost interest in his studies and life in general. In the intervening years I often thought about what became of him, but sadly he joined the long list of acquaintances who I never laid eyes on again.

After we had reminisced about Dolphin Square and its tenants, Charles bizarrely recalled a story about the Queen. In 1982 the newspapers made a big fuss about a man who broke into the Queen's bedroom and was found by Her Majesty sitting on the royal bed. This level of security would be laughed at now but after attempting for five minutes to name the interloper we gave up. Not even I could remember his name.

'I wonder if that Indian restaurant still has the poster in the window of Princess Diana leaving with her takeaway,' I said.

The nursery where she worked was adjacent to St George's Square as you walked towards Pimlico tube station and the Indian restaurant where the photo originated was literally next door to the nursery. We never saw her in the flesh but I imagined her spending many hours playing hoopla and hopscotch with the children in the playground. Inevitably any discussion about Diana led to her untimely death. We all remembered exactly where we were when we heard the awful news that August day in 1997.

I recalled the eerie silence in the streets when her funeral took place, and a few days later I drove with my wife to London to see the extraordinary carpet of flowers outside Buckingham and Kensington Palaces. It must have been my melancholy mood because I felt unbearably sad as we talked about her; it seemed so unfair that she was no longer with us. Monty dragged me out of my reverie and in true Monty style, stood up, saluted and raised his glass to 'The Queen of Hearts', before he reminded us about one of our favourite haunts, somewhere perhaps Diana may have met friends for leisurely lunch before her royal courtship and her life changed forever.

In the evenings our girlfriends worked at a bistro in Churton Street. It was called Grumbles and had a blue awning and a cozy alpine chalet feel. According to Monty it was still going strong today. We began a competition to see how many dishes we could remember from the menu. After five minutes it was evident there was only one winner, a dish that continued to send our taste buds into sensory overload. I closed my eyes, inhaled deeply and experienced the familiar nasal rush from the crust of hot English mustard and brown sugar. The Grumbles Filet.

It was a dish we had enjoyed on countless occasions and brought back happy memories of wine-laden meals in the snug wood panelled basement. Charles constantly tried to butt in. It was evident he was desperate to regale us with a story of his own; regrettably the wine and spirits were making his dyslexia worsen. His thoughts and speech floundered as he tried to find the right words. In the end, sensing his frustration, Monty and I shut up and let him speak, but time was running out and I sensed my opportunity for a final denouement was slipping away.

In our final year we embarked on an ambitious food project. It was to be our gastronomic tour de force and naturally Charles took control of it from day one. It consisted of a seven course tasting menu, with wines to complement each course. Something which you see quite often now, but back then it was in its infancy, like the nouvelle cuisine we were all being influenced by.

It had been Charles' idea to base the theme on a book by David Thorpe entitled 'Rude Food.' The idea of linking food and sex could only have come from Charles' warped mind and he spent many hours leafing through the book before producing his final menu. It consisted of: consommé with pasta letters, where the guests were encouraged to make rude words; an entrée of asparagus spears served with Hollandaise Sauce; a fish course of oysters and fillets of Dover Sole delicately sculpted to resemble...well, you can guess; a main course of muscle-bound Steak Tartare; and for dessert the tried and tested flambéed bananas in cognac.

He was exceptionally proud of his pièce de résistance. It was served in the famous Escoffier Room and at the end of the meal, amongst much fanfare, an attractive first year girl was wheeled in on a trolley. She was covered in a plethora of exotic fruits surrounded by small pots of Chantilly cream. In her beige body-stocking with her symmetrical black bob she reminded me of Cleopatra. Dessert was never seen the same way again.

Charles turned to me rather than Monty. 'What was her name? Spunky girl and she didn't complain once.'

'Alex,' I said.

Charles jaw dropped. 'Bloody hell how do you do that?'

Monty fiddled with his cuffs.

I shrugged my shoulders. 'I just can,' I replied.

'Fuck me, you should be on Mastermind with a memory like that.'

I didn't want to be drawn into a long-winded discussion about my long-term memory capabilities, I needed a diversion.

All the food talk alerted my stomach to its current state of emptiness and I asked for menus from a passing waitress. When they arrived I noticed that Charles was squinting and having trouble reading the small print with his one good eye. I attempted to be helpful.

'Do you want me to order for you?' I asked.

'As long as it's not sausages, mash and cabbage.'

Monty agreed that he also never wanted to eat that meal again and chose a Thai curry. I peered over the top of my menu at Charles.

'Do you trust me to order for you?'

He placed his menu on the floor. 'I trust you...' He paused. '...although we put our trust in you once and look what happened.'

My shoulders slumped in defeat. He always found a way to keep the upper hand.

I remembered the dinner party in question. After the meal someone had passed me a small foil package. So off I went to the toilets. I sat on the seat and opened the pouch. I retrieved my Barclaycard form my wallet and started cutting the powder into lines on the seat. Luckily I had a ten pound note. I rolled it up, leant forward and held it over the first line. I remember thinking at the time that there seemed to be a lot of lines. Then I snorted. The first line disappeared. My eyes watered, then I snorted again, and again, and again until the foil was empty.

Ten minutes later I walked back to the dining room. My head was spinning, so much I thought I might throw up. In fact five minutes later I did. I remembered everyone watched me stagger back to my seat.

The host looked mortified. 'How many lines did you do?'

I bowed my head. 'All of them,' I replied

Charles sneered. 'And that was why you weren't invited again. Clever boy put the whole evening's entertainment up his nose.'

Charles nudged my arm and excused himself, muttering something about a drug addiction. I could tell he was smirking.

'I need a piss before we eat.'

Monty squeezed out of the booth at the same time. He turned to me and very much tongue-in-cheek announced to everyone nearby that he would lend Charles a hand. I watched them scrimmage on the way to the toilets as Charles tried with his one good hand to fend off Monty's attempts to ruffle his hair, something Charles hated.

While they were away from the table I methodically scanned the menu again. The waitress returned to take the order and I ordered two *Boeuf Bourguignon* and a green chicken curry for Monty, with a side of Jasmine rice and French bread for us. I hoped Charles would be pleasantly surprised by my retro choice. He had cooked it enough times for us at Winchester Street over the years and it was a meal I knew he particularly enjoyed.

The cute waitress in a miniskirt followed Charles and Monty back to the table and announced glumly that the kitchen was unable to take any more orders. This news did not go down well, especially with Charles. He was about to embark on a visit to the kitchen but something made him change his mind and instead, with great effort, he retrieved a ten pound note from his wallet and placed it provocatively in the waitress' apron. There followed a brief exchange as the waitress enquired as to how he got his injuries. Charles, clearly enjoying her attention, moved his good hand to within inches of her shapely behind, but wisely withdrew it at the last second. The waitress, oblivious to how close she came to being felt up, smiled sweetly and with a seductive sway of her hips, which appeared to be only for Charles' benefit, hurried off to another table. He sat there with a smug 'I told you I still have it' look etched on his face and I laid a wager with Monty that our food order would now be fulfilled.

While we waited to see who would win the wager I showed Charles the photographs. He drooled over his impersonation of Boy George and then became noticeably moved by the photograph of all of us having lunch in the Alps. It was a snapshot of youth, a moment in time perfectly captured by the lens. Monty, John and I sat in a row while Charles once again took centre stage as he lay in the snow at our feet. It looked like a still from a pop video, four good-looking twenty year olds with white teeth, big hair and attitude.

The photograph seemed to have a calming effect on Charles.

'Can I keep it? I have so few of John from around that time.'

I placed it carefully in the breast pocket of his shirt.

'Here, all yours.'

I thought he was about to add something more, but instead he regarded both of us in that way he had when he desperately wanted to be like us, but knew he couldn't be. He simply nodded twice and smiled. The smile was a little forced but I understood that my gesture was appreciated.

Needless to say the food arrived, which left me and Monty in no doubt that the waitress had fallen for the charms of the leery one-armed man sitting at our table. The waitress served Charles last and his eye lingered a little too long on the girl's cleavage as she leant across him. She didn't seem the least inhibited, in fact her reaction was quite the opposite and she skipped away with a flick of her perfect fringe. Some things never change, I reflected.

Charles still had it and we didn't.

Charles peered distastefully at his plate. I looked at the steaming plate of stew and couldn't see anything wrong, unless Charles had suddenly become a vegetarian in the last few minutes and that seemed highly unlikely. He pushed it away with a trembling hand.

I looked for assistance from Monty, but the blood had drained from his tanned face. Charles was clearly struggling with something. He looked like he had seen a ghost.

In an attempt to try and fathom what exactly was wrong I leant over and dunked a chunk of French bread in his bowl. I popped the dripping piece of bread into my mouth. The rich Burgundian sauce infused with thyme, garlic and smoked pancetta was hot and tasty. I smacked my lips; it was delicious and exactly like mine.

I was confused. 'What's wrong?' I asked.

Charles paused. I could tell he was weighing things up in his mind and something unsaid passed between him and Monty.

'I've lost my appetite,' he snapped.

Monty stopped eating his curry. I hadn't a clue what was going on. All I saw was a perfectly good plate of *Boeuf Bourguignon* going to waste.

I was convinced the joke was at my expense.

'Come on, don't arse about, there's nothing wrong with it,' I said.

Charles didn't reply. I was unnerved. He had not moved a muscle and was clearly vexed.

'Don't tell me I ordered the wrong meal, I thought I was being clever by ordering one of your favourites. You used to cook it for us in Winchester Street. Don't you remember?'

Monty put his cutlery down and muttered to himself under his breath. I felt a rush of nervous energy and my left hand began to twitch.

*Something was clearly wrong.*

Charles glanced at me and perhaps it was my imagination, but there was something in that look, not hostility, but something else: remorse or guilt. I gnawed nervously on the fat cuticle around the nail on my index finger. Charles looked down repeatedly at his plate.

'Monty was there. I bet he can remember what he ate that night.'

Monty seemed to physically shrink. He bowed his head and I could feel the tension between us, it was palpable. I waited for Monty to push his food away, just like Charles had done.

Charles inhaled deeply, holding the air down in his lungs. His jaw locked, his features hardened like granite. I sensed something lurking in the shadows but I was afraid to look.

I looked at Monty, then at Charles, and my world tilted.

# CHARLES' STORY
## July 1984

I leaned forward, my mind like an enigma machine attempting to decipher a complex code. Charles cleared his throat. The timbre in his voice deepened. It had lost all its earlier spark. While Monty disconsolately picked at his food, Charles began to recount the events of that night.

'It had been a blisteringly hot day and the temperature hadn't dropped much by evening. Monty and I decided to go to Grumbles for an early meal. It was pre-arranged that John would pick us up afterwards in the Limo and drive us to Baz and Annie's. We didn't think you'd mind if we were a bit late. Anyhow, we were starving and when we got there the restaurant was buzzing. The last exam was over and we were in high spirits: Freedom and an entire summer of parties lay ahead. I ordered *Boeuf Bourguignon*, it was delicious. Monty had the steak, what a surprise. We drank a bottle of red…'

Charles put the fingers of his good hand to his lips and kissed them.

'Bon appétit.' His tone was self-mocking.

I sat in stunned silence, my hands in my lap. My own plate of food also grew cold in front of me. I had no idea where all this was going.

Charles lowered his voice. 'We never made it. But you know that. '

I felt the need to speak now but my voice wavered, unsteady.

'I waited all night and you didn't bloody show up. We hadn't argued. It didn't make any sense. You didn't make any effort to contact me, what was I supposed to think?'

Charles asked for his plate to be removed. He told the waitress the painkillers were making him feel unwell. He dabbed beads of sweat off his forehead with a napkin.

'It would have been easy now, send a text, call from your mobile. We were going to explain everything to you. Well, as much as we were allowed under the circumstances, but events just moved so quickly. Everyone moved on, Mel and I moved away. I sent you an invitation to my wedding and then I found out you were on the other side of the world.'

Charles was not making sense. 'Under the

circumstances! What the hell does that mean?'

Charles toyed with a book of matches.

'Shh, let's all calm down. I need to start at the beginning. I need to tell you about my twin.'

I sat back and defensively folded my arms. 'Ok, go ahead.'

'John finished University that summer, he gained a 1$^{st}$ in Business and Economics, clever bastard, and while he waited for the job of a lifetime to materialise he secured a full-time position as a driver for a Limo company. I think it came from a rowing contact, one of his school chums. The company had a number of high profile clients on its books and John had to be vetted by a security firm before he could start. It was a highly responsible job and paid well, especially when you took into account the undeclared tips.'

'I arranged for him to come to Grumbles and take us to Baz and Annie's. I can't remember the exact timings now, but I reckoned we finished eating around 8pm. John had a no-show and arrived early so he parked the Limousine right outside the bistro and came in to hurry us along. The blacked-out windows caused a stir and a few of the customers sitting outside gave in to their curiosity and tried to peer inside.'

'When John strolled in, smart suit, dark glasses, his hat tucked under his arm, customers stopped eating and heads turned, especially the women. It was like a scene from An Officer and A Gentleman. I persuaded John to have a couple of glasses of wine before we set off, which caused a heated argument between the three of us. John never drank on duty but I wouldn't let it go, even when I knew how important his job was. I can be a selfish sod sometimes.'

I shivered. I recalled the eye witness accounts of Princess Diana's last hours and Henry Paul, the chauffeur, drinking in the Parisian hotel bar and the fateful consequences they all suffered later. I feared what was coming next.

Charles gathered himself and continued.

'The plan was to meet up with you, have a few drinks at Baz and Annie's and then move on to a nightclub. John was on call for most of the night but he said if he knew which club we were going to be at, he would drive by later and give us a lift back to Winchester Street. We would get the full V.I.P. treatment.'

'The girls had the night off. I was pissed off because I

had to pay for the wine. Anyhow we left Grumbles and piled into the Limo. It was muggy outside and John put the air conditioning on as we drove west along sidestreets towards Ebrury Bridge and Belgravia. We drove past the Ebrury Wine Bar which was jammed full of city types celebrating the end of the working week, then turned into Ebrury Street and headed towards Sloane Square. As we approached the crossroads with Eaton Terrace a man stepped out into the road.

'He didn't look.'

I felt like I was in a plummeting lift that kept falling and falling. When it finally stopped, I was strangely taken back to my own preparations earlier that same evening. I had seen my girlfriend off at Victoria Station. Her parents lived in Sussex and she was going home to ask them if they would allow her to come to Australia with me later on in the summer. I returned to Winchester Street around 7pm to pack up the last of my belongings. We had been gradually sifting through all our stuff and now only a few bags remained in the hall. Monty had taken his kit to St. George's Square, where the girls' lease had longer to run. Charles meanwhile had the boot of his Mini and a secret cupboard at Mel's flat for his storage needs. Hanging clothes in wardrobes was a risky business in the event her father made an impromptu visit.

I was dreading the next day when, no doubt with an almighty hangover, I would have to go through the inventory with the agent prior to our deposits being released. After which, Charles was supposed to be driving us down to Kent for a final whirlwind tour of the Home Counties and numerous parties. Our final drunken hurrah.

I recalled how Charles and Monty hadn't showed the least smidgen of interest in the whole flat leaving process and the possible forfeiture of their deposits. As usual the finer details were all down to me. There were keys missing and I made a mental note to check with Charles when we met up at Baz and Annie's later. He never returned anything; he never saw the point. Objects like that had no value for him, but I was sure the deposit money would lure him back to reality.

I wanted to vacate the property with the minimum of fuss, unlike our enforced night-time departure from Avonmore Road. I moved from room to room, my eye roving over furniture and soft furnishings for tell-tale burn marks or stains. A reek of stale beer and tobacco and something unsavoury washed over me. I tried a window, but they were all locked shut and I couldn't find a key. I opened the door to the bathroom. It was the only room that smelled vaguely clean. I ran a finger over a mottled glass shelf and decided enough was enough; I wasn't in the mood to do any more window dressing. I retrieved my wash bag, showered and took a taxi to Baz and Annie's.

# THE CADILLAC

There followed a prolonged period of silence, each of us caught up in our own recollections of that evening. Eventually I spoke.

'Hold on. Let me get this right. You were all in John's limousine and you ran someone down?'

My voice was shrill, and incredulous. I didn't have all the facts but my imagination sparked a vivid image of the crash scene: the Limousine, my friends riding in the back, the sickening sound of shattered flesh and bone. The Limousine in question was a Black Cadillac, large grill and tinted windows. Charles helped me out with the finer details. He said it was a very smart car, the sort of car Presidents got shot in.

I observed Charles. His good hand shook. 'Someone died.'

'Jesus!'

For a moment that was all I could say. Then anger replaced my consternation.

*Monty knew.*

I shook my head in disbelief. John was dead and only now did Charles in his infinite wisdom feel it was time to break down the dam. I tried unsuccessfully to quash the anger that simmered close to the surface.

'I don't know who or what to believe anymore.'

Charles grabbed my hand and whispered in my ear. 'Do you think I would make something like that up?' His face was half lit and demons danced across his silhouetted face.

'Jesus, I think I need a cigarette,' I said.

Charles beckoned over the waitress. She was hovering nearby, waiting for another chance to make an impression with her girly charm and D cup cleavage.

'I'll get us some.'

The waitress returned with a packet of Silk Cut and we all went outside. Charles offered up the packet and from his breast pocket withdrew a book of matches with a grinning monkey logo on the sleeve. I drew long and hard on my cigarette, pulling the nicotine deep down in my lungs until I thought I might choke or spew. I hadn't smoked for years and my head spun.

We stood out on the pavement. Alderley Edge High Street was busy, groups of people moving from bar to bar. I felt the warmth from the patio heater on my back, but outside the bar we were alone; no-one else wanted to brave the cool night air for too long. I watched the staff through the window. Someone pointed in our direction. I didn't think we had been that loud, but Charles had that effect on people, they wanted to provoke him, even if they didn't know him.

Charles lit another smoke and passed it to Monty, but he waved it away. Charles dropped the smoldering cigarette and ground it under his shoe. Monty shuffled uncomfortably from one foot to another; he looked unwell.

The nicotine calmed me little. I attempted to blow a smoke ring but failed miserably. I was out of practice.

'You've lived with this, all this time.' It was a statement rather than a question.

However it didn't adequately explain why they had broken off all contact. In a split-second my supposedly loyal friends had drawn a line in the sand and banished me like a man with leprosy. It didn't make any sense.

Charles leant his injured arm on a trough full of vibrant spring flowers, his body bent over like a hunchback. There was no apology. I suppose I wasn't expecting one. It sounded unfair but I hoped these events came back to haunt him. I watched him drag hard on the cigarette and his breathing became laboured as he exhaled. I could tell he wasn't enjoying it.

'It was a nightmare. Our nightmare,' he croaked.

My hackles rose.

'Do you expect me feel sorry for you? Isn't this why we are all here this evening? To hear the truth?'

Charles shrugged his shoulders and ground out his cigarette with a Gucci heel. He cocked his head at Monty. His tone was brusque.

'We need to go back in, this is going to take a while.'

I followed Charles back inside, while Monty deliberately hung back in the shadows. He was clearly distracted by something. He eventually reappeared but I sensed an inner struggle. I wouldn't have been the least surprised if he had walked off into the night and disappeared again.

We returned to our table in the corner. After a brief interlude Charles ordered an expensive bottle of Scotch and a pitcher of ice. He poured a generous measure into each tumbler. I was concerned. The vast cocktail of alcohol and painkillers Charles had consumed over the last few hours made him more and more unpredictable. Like a chameleon he changed again, shifting from an almost catatonic state to a mass of manic energy. In a hushed tone he resumed the harrowing story, his good eye never still, like it had a mind of its own.

'The man appeared from nowhere and stumbled into the road. John wouldn't have seen him until it was too late. The impact sent him somersaulting over the Cadillac. It was a sickening sound as he bounced off the roof and landed in the road behind us. John pulled over and heaved on the handbrake.'

'The world around us carried on in slow motion. For the first few seconds John didn't move, then he began to pummel the steering wheel over and over again with his fists. The sound was muffled by the glass screen. A minute passed before he retracted the partition. John shouted at us, he told us to get out, he would deal with it. We were never in the Cadillac. I remember his eyes, they were dark windows of terror.'

'We were in a state of shock but we did as we were told and slipped out onto the pavement. The streets were relatively quiet considering how warm the evening was. I remembered a lady walking her dog on the other side of the road. She stopped to look at the Cadillac mounted on the pavement, but she couldn't see us crouched down beside the vehicle.'

'I saw the crumpled shape of a man. He lay close to the kerb about 20 metres behind us. There was blood on the windshield, while up front John sat frozen in his seat, eyes closed. We watched a passing cyclist jump off his bike and run over to the lifeless body and further down the road somebody else ran to a red phone box. I feared the worst but at this point I didn't know he was dead. I found out later He never regained consciousness and was pronounced dead on arrival at Westminster Hospital.'

'I grabbed Monty's arm and we darted down an alleyway. We needed to get as far as away as quickly as possible and I hoped no-one had seen us. We ran like Coe and Ovett, like our lives depended on it. After a few minutes we caught our breath and walked out of the alleyway into the shaded backstreets. I pulled Monty along and we headed across Pimlico towards St George's Square.'

John would tell them later that, shortly after the incident happened, the police arrived in a white Transit and closed the road. Moments later an ambulance arrived. While the medics tried desperately to resuscitate the man lying in the road, John sat dazed and shaking on a bench and waited for a policeman to return with a breathalyzer. To his relief the roadside breath test was negative, but along with two eye witnesses John was asked to accompany the officers back to Rochester Row Police Station to give statements.

The scene of crime team arrived next in a smaller van. The men and women in white suits began unloading cases of forensic equipment. They photographed the Cadillac from all angles, took measurements and over the course of the next few hours made their assessments. When they were finished the Cadillac was loaded onto a low-loader and removed for further tests at the police pound.

Charles threw two ice cubes into his glass and the level rose half way up the tumbler. I sat with my chin cradled in my hands and listened as the story accelerated. I didn't want to break the spell.

'Monty and I headed towards Victoria Station where the roads and pavements were busier. We turned left over Ecclestone Bridge and walked along Belgrave Road. I told Monty to stop looking over his shoulder and walk as normally as possible. We were just two students going to the pub for a drink. I was confident that if we made it to St George's Square we would be safe.'

'The walk took an eternity and every police siren set our pulses racing. I deliberated about phoning my parents but I didn't want to compromise myself. They would hear soon enough and they were in a much better position to help John. I knew we had to distance ourselves from the accident and as we walked I told Monty we needed to get our stories straight. I put on my bravest face, but underneath my calm exterior I was shitting myself because I knew it was entirely possible we had been seen as we slipped out of the Cadillac. Then it wouldn't matter what kind of attempt we made at a cover-up, we were done for. If that was the case and we could be identified, the police might have been able to trace us to our flat. It was unlikely, but it was feasible and it was the main reason for not going home to Winchester Street.'

'We walked up the steps of number 64 and rang the bell. A few seconds later the door clicked open and we slipped in. On the way up to the second floor I realised we had to come up with a cover story for the girls. It would be one of many lies I would tell over the coming weeks and months.'

'I pushed Monty into a bathroom and locked the door. I talked and Monty listened: we ate at Grumbles but we never hitched a ride with John. I made him repeat it over and over again. To avoid suspicion I decided to tell the girls we had come to give them new directions to the party in Kent. I told the girls we were going to get a bus to the King's Road and meet you at Baz and Annie's. I had to explain to Monty it was difficult to trace people who travelled by bus as opposed to getting a cab. There was no CCTV on buses back then and cab bookings could be traced. I made Monty swear on his mother's life to stick to my version of events. We spent an hour with the girls, who thankfully never suspected anything was wrong.'

'Monty's head was in a spin and he didn't really understand the gravity of the situation we now found ourselves in. He kept asking me why we weren't going to Baz and Annie's. I had to explain it over and over again. I was second-guessing everything and I wasn't sure what would happen to us if it came out we were travelling illegally in John's Cadillac. However that wasn't what worried me the most. We had left the scene of an accident and I remembered reading somewhere that a custodial sentence was not out of the question.'

'We needed to lie low, re-group, let the dust settle for a while. In the end it was an easy decision. I persuaded Monty to leave with me for Kent that night. Our getaway was made easier because my Mini was parked nearby in a sidestreet. Mel and Tash were away somewhere warm and exotic with their father. To kill some more time we went to a local pub and waited until closing, then we drove out of London and headed south to Kent.'

Charles sat back. I thought he had finished, but after a brief pause he spoke again.

'My mind raced through all manner of permutations and outcomes, none of them good. My immediate thoughts were obviously with my brother, but part of me was wrapped up in my own self-preservation. I just didn't know if I was making the right decisions but as usual it was all down to me because Monty clearly wasn't up to it.'

Monty looked like someone had slapped his face. Charles could be such a cold bastard sometimes.

'Later that night we arrived at Steve's farmhouse. When people asked where you were I told everyone you had blown us out and gone home with your girlfriend. It was perfectly believable: you'd blown us out before.'

He was right. I had no means of transport after I had been banned for drink-driving the previous year. My girlfriend didn't drive and if I wasn't with Charles and Monty then I probably wasn't going to Kent.

In the sanctity of our corner booth, Charles with his one good eye willed me to believe what he had told me. I suppose I did, but it didn't change how I felt inside. I had been dispensable: cruel but true. I felt rejected and the hollowness returned. Charles of course was oblivious to my hurt and continued with a sketchy portrayal of John's arrest.

'John was interviewed at great length by the police. When the tests revealed he was below the drink-drive limit he thought he was going to walk out a free man. However it was during this process that the police's attention was drawn to an irregularity with his driving licence. John was so thorough in everything he did it was unthinkable he hadn't checked, but it appeared the hire company had goofed up big time.'

'After thinking the worst was over the police advised John to enlist the aid of a solicitor because they were charging him with a motoring offence. To this day John felt they were looking for something to pin on him, any small infringement that would allow them to charge him. The police were different back then, maybe they were jealous of him.'

'He gave his personal details, his flat address in Putney, next of kin and the details of the company he worked for. He expected a company representative to come to the station but no-one came. In the end he phoned our parents, who made the late night trek to London. In the early hours, still dressed in his uniform, he walked out of Rochester Row, shaken and unsure about what battles lay ahead.'

'Our parents were concerned that he might have suffered permanent psychological scars. PTSD to give it its correct title. John was only twenty-four; his whole life had been turned upside down in a split second. Our father was well-connected and once John was home he enlisted the assistance of a good lawyer who persuaded John to attend regular counselling sessions.'

I was perched on the edge of my seat.

'So did he get off?' I asked

Charles raised an eyebrow.

'His defence team provided the court with a whole

host of glowing character references, from old school masters, work colleagues and family friends. One of whom happened to be a judge. John pleaded guilty and after a short trial he was given a means-tested fine and points on his licence. The family breathed a collective sigh of relief, but there was little to celebrate and, shortly after, our father set about pursuing the owners of the Limousine hire company. However memories of that night haunted him. His unblemished character had a permanent stain. Even his wife and closest friends were unaware of the inner struggle that continued from that day right to the very end.'

'And you and Monty?' I asked.

Charles avoided my gaze.

'We kept our heads down until it was all over.'

I sensed there was more, but he became less coherent and slumped against a pillar. I felt only anguish and heartache for John, and as for the other two…

I wanted to know everything, every little sordid detail.

## 'LET'S MISBEHAVE'

I leant back and took a thoughtful slug of peaty whisky. I looked to my left and right and saw my friends through different eyes. I started to trawl through the events surrounding that night. I went back to the beginning. We were about to be unleashed on the world. We were men but not quite there, not the real deal.

We looked to the future, making our mark, grown-up jobs, mortgages, children perhaps, but inside, deep in our hearts the wildness still remained, an ocean of restless dark water. Then there had been a dreadful accident and everything had changed for all of us.

This massive catastrophe must have skewed the privileged worlds that Charles and Monty inhabited. Here, tonight, I saw with my own eyes the ramifications of such a life-changing tragedy. I couldn't for one moment imagine living with such a dark secret. It would tear me up until eventually I broke apart, my physical body left as a mere empty husk. Would the secret have remained hidden if John hadn't died? Perhaps; sometimes ignorance was preferable to the truth, I thought.

I couldn't condone their actions and deliberated about how I would have reacted if I had been in the Limousine that night. I was damn sure I would have panicked, blanked out the entire outside world and screamed for my mother, like I had when I watched a car run over our dog. There was no way on this earth I would have been as focused as Charles, but did that excuse him from what happened afterwards, the dubious decisions and the lengthy wall of silence?

But why had Charles chosen this evening? One never knew how the machinery of his mind worked. It was never based on real emotions and rarely structured. I toyed with the photograph of us in Meribel, observing the fresh tanned faces and perfectly white teeth. I thought of John in his prime. This evening was not really about us: it was about him and his life. His life before the crash and his life afterwards, after the court case.

I only knew him as Charles' brother, I couldn't say we were close friends, but I would do anything to take us all back to those unburdened times, undo what had happened. Unlike the other two of course, I could, it was my secret gift. I focused on a far off pin-prick of light and even though they were inches away Charles and

Monty were completely oblivious to my reverie.

I heard the voices, the tribal chants, the laughter. I felt the spring sun on my face, snowflakes caught in the wind. I could smell the factor 25, taste the lip-balm and a hint of aniseed spirit on my lips from the previous night. It was as clear as mountain air. John was the thread and through him, our lives, although completely separate, were all magically joined. How strange it was that one momentous event all those years ago should bring us to this place tonight.

When I turned back Charles was snoring: the booze and painkillers had finally caught up with him. In a way it was a relief because while he was sedated we were saved from the wrecking ball that was his alter ego. Monty rubbed his face with his hands; he too looked drained. Charles did that to you.

Monty was preoccupied with resting Charles' head on a cushion. It was like the dominant force had lost all its power and I watched fascinated as the gentle giant fussed over the fallen King. He was spent, the lies and deceit throughout the intervening years had finally caught up with him. He had been unplugged, lost his control, a Samson unable to dominate the world without his great strength. Monty held up the Scotch bottle for me to see: it was nearly empty.

Monty started to say something but stopped.

'I've never seen him like this,' I whispered.

Monty sighed, his expression overflowed with resignation and sadness. He moved round to my side of the booth and put his oversized hand on mine. It was meaningful and tender, and it spoke volumes about our past and the individual journeys we had taken since we parted.

Monty gestured with his hands, like a priest at the pulpit. 'So here we are again. Just the two of us. I wish I could turn the clock back I really do. I would have done things differently.'

I sat transfixed. His touch carried a strange hypnotic power, something that had lain dormant until Charles fell asleep.

Monty kept his hand on mine.

'I'm not blameless and I feel guilty about a lot of things that went on back then. If I'm being totally honest none of it makes any sense now, but I think you were better off not being involved because living with these lies has taken its toll.'

Monty carefully repositioned Charles' plaster cast.

'As you can see.'

His utter frankness moved me. My eyes misted over and my chest heaved.

'I'm not here to judge you,' I said. 'I want to know.'

It was all I could say. It was like we were back in Winchester Street, the two of us sitting on a garden bench sipping gin and tonics as Monty recounted a recent skirmish we had been involved in, like the time Monty slept with a stuffed bear at Gordon's party. That night I had consumed more than my fair share of red wine and as the others tucked into a hearty breakfast I felt my body begin to shut down. I thought I was dying and Charles hailed a cab. We only made it as far as Hyde Park because there was a CND march blocking our route back to Pimlico. The cab driver let us out. They dragged me across the park allowing me to drink like a dog from various fountains as we headed home.

Eventually we made it back to Winchester Street. I made a miraculous recovery from a bout of alcohol poisoning and returned to a nearby pub that evening. Monty meanwhile had no recollection of an extravagant purchase he made on the walk back, his monthly credit card statement the only proof that he was now the owner of the latest Salomon touring skis.

Monty smiled and placed his giant hand on my arm.

'I remember the bear now.'

He stared at me for what seemed an eternity. 'Listen. I need to apologise for not making more effort, but you know what Charles is like. He took control of everything. Charles says jump and you ask how high.'

I nodded. I remembered. Of course I remembered. It was part of our shared history and couldn't be changed.

I paused. 'Do you think we've changed?' I asked.

Monty considered the question carefully. He patted my head. 'Physically obviously. For a start you looked much better with hair.'

I punched his arm playfully. His mouth curled up into a smile and his eyes changed colour again.

'Yes, of course, but I think underneath the suffering and worry lines there is a small part within us, a unique bond that can never be broken.'

I nodded in agreement. I felt that too.

'I don't think we had anything to measure ourselves against when we first met, that's the difference. We just existed and found some common ground, we enjoyed each other's company and we made each other laugh. We were trailblazers and we had lived survived in a frantic existential world. I think the fact we were all different helped us co-exist without destroying each other.'

Wise words, I thought.

Monty sat up, his back military straight. 'God, you couldn't have three Charles' in the same room. There would be World War Three.'

Charles stirred and mumbled, but the words were indecipherable. I couldn't imagine him ever finding the right words.

Monty regarded me with unhealthy fascination. 'You know your problem - you over-analyse everything. Just, let it be. We all have our memories, just about, let's be satisfied with that and leave the ghosts to haunt someone else.'

He was right. I knew the truth now. I knew about John, the accident, his fall from grace. More importantly I knew what happened to Charles and Monty on that balmy evening in July, and the awful code of silence they had endured ever since.

*I knew everything.*

I looked at my watch. 1am. The bar was emptying. A few stragglers drained the last dregs from their wine glasses, while in the corner two businessmen swirled end of evening brandies. I caught the attention of a passing waitress and hailed the cabs, then as if by magic the lights around us flickered and the jazz music started up again. Monty had a faraway look in his eye. I focused on the music: it was very familiar.

'Oh my God listen.'

In an instant I was transported back to Baz and Annie's. The bar resonating to our voices as we sang along to Grace Kelly, Bing Crosby and Louis Armstrong. The three of us perched at the bar, while Baz mixed a lethal tequila-based cocktail. I recalled one of his early concoctions, Rocket Fuel, which summed up its brutal alcoholic properties very aptly.

I looked quizzically at Monty.' What are you smiling about?'

'Do you remember what it's called?'

I knew the film, I knew the words but for once my mind went blank. I couldn't remember the song title, even though I'd heard it hundreds of times.

'What is it?'

Maybe it was a trick of the light, maybe I imagined it, but all of a sudden he reverted to the Monty of old. I recalled a rugby talk he gave when he appeared in full kit, a rugby ball tucked under his arm and a yellow headband across his forehead. It was how I always remembered him.

'It's "Lets Misbehave." It sums up my life quite neatly.'

Monty shuffled along so our shoulders almost touched. In hushed tones he became the narrator once more.

'I've had to keep a secret for nearly thirty years.'

I didn't know what the hell he was talking about.

'You must swear never to breathe a word about what I am about to tell you. Not even Charles.'

I looked at the man asleep in the corner, the crumpled shirt, the ruffled hair. Saliva dribbled form a corner of his mouth.

Monty edged closer. 'Don't blame him, in his own way he wanted to protect all of us.'

# MONTY'S STORY
## July 1984

*There was more. There always was.*

'We sat at our favourite window table. The girls had been given the night off, which meant there would be no free wine and Charles was irritable. He was always thinking about his bank balance. I ordered the *Grumbles Fillet* and Charles, the *Boeuf Bourguinon,* which he washed down with a bottle of red Bordeaux. By the time the bill arrived he was flexing his muscles, his cantankerous mood had lifted and he was in full party mode.'

'Charles mentioned he had spoken to John. He said he was coming to collect us from the restaurant and drive us to Baz and Annie's. He hoped it would turn a few heads, like we had at the Summer Ball when Fiona organised a Limousine to ferry us to and from the hotel. There were only two parking spaces outside the bistro and both were occupied so John had no option but to double-park the Cadillac right outside. Even without a flag flying on the bonnet, it looked like royalty had arrived for an impromptu visit. Heads turned and one diner actually got up from his table on the pavement and tried to peer inside.'

'John made it a strict rule to never drink on duty, but Charles persuaded him to have a couple of glasses of wine before we set off. I remembered them arguing because John felt Charles had pressurised him into having a drink. It was typical Charles because John could have lost his job over a needless indiscretion like that.'

I listened patiently, waiting for him to divulge something new, but Monty's story seemed more or less the same.

'The plan had always been to have a few drinks at Baz and Annie's and then move on to a nightclub. John was on call but he said if he knew which club we were going to end up at, he would drive by later and see if we needed a lift back to Winchester Street.'

Monty cleared his throat. 'There was someone else.'

It took a second or two for me to digest what he had said. I asked him to repeat it.

'There was someone else in the Cadillac,' he said.

I raised an eyebrow. 'Who?'

'A friend.'

'Male, female?'

Monty's tone was brusque. 'A guy.'

I was stunned. Why hadn't Charles told the truth?

'Ok.' I said, still not seeing why it was important.

'This guy was a paying client.'

I followed Monty's train of thought. This guy was in the Cadillac when John arrived at Grumbles and if he didn't get out then he was still there when…A nervous tick developed in my jaw, but I kept absolutely still. I feared he would change his mind and stop talking if I flinched. I felt like I had when my son was born, my body suspended above the table, an observer to the conversation below.

'The three of us rode in the back of the Cadillac. The evening was warm and as the car headed west alongside streets towards Belgravia, I remembered feeling cocooned in air conditioned comfort. It was a pleasant surprise after the oppressive heat of Grumbles. John piped the stereo through to the rear compartment. It was thoroughly decadent, there were champagne flutes and a bottle of Krug on ice.'

'John drove past the Ebrury Wine Bar. City types in pinstripe suits spilled out onto the pavement as they celebrated the end of the working week. We turned into

Ebrury Street and headed towards Sloane Square. As we approached the crossroads with Eaton Terrace a man stepped out into the road.'

Monty shook his head. 'John never saw him until it was too late.'

'We heard the impact, it was a sickening sound, but we had no idea what John had hit. He pulled over and stopped the car. We observed him through the glass partition. I will never forget those moments in the Limousine, when the world slowed down. John sat very still for a few seconds and then the world sped up again as he pummelled the steering wheel with both hands.'

'The glass muffled his screams but we knew instinctively something terrible had happened. My immediate reaction was that John had hit a large dog. A minute passed before he retracted the glass partition. He told Charles and I to get out of the car immediately. He would deal with it.'

'So you were all in the Cadillac when the fatality occurred?'

My own head was in a spin as I tried to digest all the information.

The stress in Monty's voice was all too evident as he

repeated 'Yes, but *we* shouldn't have been there,' over and over again.

I was confused and frustrated, but I didn't want Monty to crack under the pressure. I needed him to calm down. I focused on my breathing and spoke in a more sympathetic tone. 'So what happened to this guy? Surely he didn't bolt with you. It was his ride.'

'No he stayed put, of course. It was only Charles and I who jumped and ran.'

Monty clasped his hands together, but he couldn't prevent them from shaking.

'We were never there. We were never there,' he sobbed.

It sounded like a movie trailer and I sounded like a suspicious cop. 'Tell me about this other guy? He was simply in the wrong place at the wrong time, wasn't he?'

Monty thought long and hard before answering. 'It all happened so quickly no-one had a chance to discuss anything. I remember John's eyes though, unblinking, strong, determined. "Don't worry" he mouthed.'

I looked across at Charles. Why did his account differ to Monty's? Charles stirred and coughed. I feared he would wake up and Monty would clam up.

*Come on Monty, hurry up.*

He sipped his water and gathered himself. 'We slipped out onto the pavement. The streets were relatively quiet. I remember a lady walking her dog on the other side of the road. It was a large poodle with a bloody pink coat on. She couldn't see us because we were crouched down beside the Cadillac. I saw the body lying in the road some distance away. I could see there was blood on the windshield and I knew he was dead. A man jumped off his bike and ran over to the lifeless body, while somebody else ran to a phone box. In those vital minutes Charles took control. We darted down an alleyway hoping no-one had seen us. After a few minutes we stopped running and walked out of an alleyway into the backstreets. It was Charles' idea to head across town towards St George's Square.'

Monty took a breath, his voice lowered. 'We needed to get as far away as quickly as possible.'

'So what happened to John and this other guy?' I asked.

Monty shrugged his shoulders helplessly. 'They sat in the car and waited for the police and ambulance to arrive.'

'And…?' I urged Monty on.

'The walk took an eternity and every police siren set our pulses racing. Charles emphasised that we had to distance ourselves from the accident and as we walked across Pimlico he began to formulate the cover story. It depended on whether we had been seen leaving the Limousine, because if that was the case and we could be identified, the police may be able to trace us to the flat. Charles explained if that was the case it was game over. He made me swear on my mother's life that I would stick to his version of events.'

I bet he did, I said, under my breath.

'Charles wasn't sure what would happen to us if it came out we were travelling illegally in John's Cadillac. However what worried him the most was that we had left the scene of an accident. He remembered reading somewhere that you could go to prison. I thought he was over-reacting but Charles said we needed to lie low for a while, re-group, let the dust settle.'

'So you left for Kent that night.'

Monty drank more water. 'Exactly.'

I was slowly but surely finding the missing pieces to the puzzle, but I felt there was still more to come.

I stared intensely at Monty. 'Why didn't Charles want me to know any of this?'

Monty was ashen. 'Charles thought it would end up in the papers.'

I looked perplexed; Monty obviously hadn't understood the question. He was close to breaking down and I backed off a little. I kept my sentences short and measured. 'It was a genuine accident. John hadn't been charged with drunk-driving so I doubt the tabloids would have found it very newsworthy. It wasn't a hit-and-run.'

Monty picked at a loose strand on his shirt. 'This guy knew me, knew us. He was going to come to Baz and Annie's. We were going to introduce him to you. We wanted to see the look on your face.'

I began to feel uneasy again. 'Hang on, back track a little here. Why did you want to see the look on my face? You said John's fare was known to you. Who was he?'

Monty shook his head. 'We were all sworn to secrecy, even John. Charles will kill me, if he…'

I raised my voice. I was angry now. 'Tell me about this other fucking man!'

Charles stirred.

'Keep your voice down,' Monty whispered.

He grimaced and rubbed his temples. He looked like he was about to get another headache.

'Here.' I passed him an ice cube and waited.

'I had known him for years.' He gave me a strange look, like there was something he desperately needed me to understand.

'He was well connected and he fixed everything. That's all you need to know.'

'Is he still alive?'

'I'm not saying any more,' Monty mumbled as his chin drooped onto his chest and his gentle giant hands squeezed the sides of his head.

'Why, it was years ago. What does it matter now?'

'It matters because back then he was a household name.'

Monty sighed and slowly raised his head. He looked across at Charles and then at me. 'I know this is difficult for you to believe but I can't tell you.'

'Can't or won't?' I pressed.

Monty fell silent and stared at an iridescent light hanging from the ceiling.

'You all covered it up. Why?'

Monty stared back. He was shutting down. My

stomach flipped.

'Don't do this to me.'

# THE THIRD PASSENGER

The accident and court case were just the beginning. However devastating it must have been for all concerned, John's involvement in the cover-up was harder to envisage. Stories like this happened to other people, other people in the news. How do you keep something like that from your family and friends? It must have tormented him every day of his life.

I recalled the story about Charles and Mel's wedding and surmised that John may not have been in the right state of mind to deal with the huge responsibility asked of him that day. I was surprised the wedding went ahead at all but perhaps they were all just playing the game, pretending everything was normal. At least it explained why Monty was best man at Charles' wedding.

Which left two crucial questions unanswered: who was this mystery man and what was his relationship with Monty? I knew Monty's and Charles' families were well-connected and initially all manner of celebrities and royalty sprang to mind. I wasn't exactly sure how wide to cast the net and deliberated over famous men in sport, radio, TV and theatre. As we sat waiting for the cabs to arrive I let my imagination run riot and fantasised about spies and directors of clandestine government departments that were all housed nearby.

I even wondered if at some time I had met this person, but the more I racked my brain the further away I got from a sensible answer. It was frustrating the hell out of me and I hated second guessing, but I concluded that this faceless man Monty described, must have been a significant pillar of the establishment. It was all slightly scary, plausible stuff, if as Monty said this man had such influence that he fixed everything. In the end I gave up because the list was endless and it was making my head spin.

Monty avoided all eye contact, constantly checking his phone for messages. He clearly wasn't going to expand any further on the subject. I was disappointed but not surprised that Monty had been 'got at' and in need of some space I excused myself and left him to babysit Charles. He looked up sheepishly and said he would chase up the taxis.

I slid out from under the table and headed for the washroom. The sinks were deep porcelain basins with harsh steel faucets. I ran the cold tap and splashed water over my face. I went and sat in a cubicle and tried to organise my thoughts before I went back upstairs. Before Charles woke up.

I couldn't stop myself thinking about the other passenger and how his control and influence in the events that unfolded that night could not be underestimated. If Monty's recollection of events was correct this man would, along with John, have gone to the Police Station to give a statement, but after that…I could only speculate. For nearly three decades they had kept his identity hidden and it had nearly destroyed them. And afterwards, who or what made them all take a vow of silence? It was like fucking James Bond or John Le Carré.

I resolutely stood up and before I left the washroom I took a long hard look at myself in the mirror. I looked no better than when I walked in a few hours ago. I drew in a deep breath and exhaled slowly. I had expected our reunion to be a sweetly painful evening, a rollercoaster of emotions, but I hadn't imagined anything on this scale. It appeared, paradoxically, that life had not run smoothly for any of us and we had all loved and lost things of value.

Especially Charles. I closed my eyes and visualised them all in the Cadillac that night. John behind the wheel, with Charles, Monty and the mysterious guest riding along in the back. All high on life but unaware of what awaited them round the next corner. I peered one last time into the past.

*Who were you?*

The silence was shattered by a hand-drier bursting into life. I swallowed an ironic laugh. If it was the truth it was some story.

# GOODBYES

Charles eventually resurfaced and opened his eyes.

'What have I missed?'

Monty put his arm round him.

'Nothing much my old friend. How are you feeling?'

Charles pressed his good hand against his ear and then pinched his nose in the manner one does after swimming underwater, or in the pressurised atmosphere of an aircraft cabin.

'You should have eaten something, you know.'

Charles' sour expression, said it all: don't lecture me.

'Taxis will be here soon,' I said breezily.

Charles stifled a yawn. 'How long have I been asleep?'

'Not long,' I lied.

'Miss anything?'

Monty coughed. I prayed Monty didn't cave in and tried not to look at him.

'No, just a few lines of a coke, a lapdance and a shooting.'

Charles didn't hear me. He could do that, tune out if required. He tucked in his shirt and waved his good hand through his hair. He slicked his eyebrow with an elegant manicured finger. The world was still spinning on its axis. He sat bolt upright, shoulders back.

'Right, we should do this again.'

Monty and I smiled at the absurdity of this larger-than-life character, in his pink Ralph Lauren shirt with matching plaster cast.

'We should,' I said enthusiastically.

Monty stood up unsteadily with his glass held at an awkward angle. 'To the "Pimlico Posse". By the way I have something to announce.'

I had no idea what was coming and looking at Charles, neither did he.

'A proposal. Every year, we must all agree to meet up on the anniversary of John's passing. The only excuse I will tolerate for non-attendance is if you stop breathing. Force majeure can not be used in your defence.'

Then under his breath, he slurred. 'More details to follow.'

I raised my glass. 'By the way, that's a pledge, not a proposal.'

Monty huffed and puffed. He looked directly at Charles.

He waved a finger. 'Whatever it is, it is not to be broken.'

I looked at the great bear of a man in front of me. His size made him a force to be reckoned with but I had never seen him ever wilfully set out to hurt anyone, unless of course it was an opposing prop in a scrum. I wished I had spent more time with him over the intervening years. In the next few days he would undoubtedly return to his solo existence and his books.

I wished him well - he didn't need anyone else to make him feel contented, he was perfectly happy being Monty, whatever that entailed, and I was proud to be his friend. I wasn't sure what other secrets Monty kept locked away, but I didn't care. I was in no position to judge him, I was hardly perfect myself.

Charles wrapped his good arm round my middle. 'Why didn't I think of that?'

Because you are a fucking selfish old sod I thought to myself, as I checked I had enough cash for the cab home, but I still love you.

'That's a great idea. We should do it in the Alps. Just like old times.'

*Just like old times*

The bill arrived. I felt a sinking feeling in my stomach. If it was split three ways I wasn't sure I had enough cash on me to pay my share. My credit card was maxed out. I was nearly broke and I said a silent prayer.

Charles checked his heaving wallet.

'I'll get this.'

I watched him drop a Black Amex card on to a silver salver. I felt like I had won the lottery.

A photo of his wife fell out alongside the credit card. He looked around guiltily before placing it back in amongst a thick wad of twenties. Charles weighed up his options.

'Mel wants a divorce. It's going to cost me a fortune.'

When he looked up his affected smile didn't reach his eyes. His words didn't shock me. I understood why he was building the cabin: he had got worse, ten times worse, and how anyone could live with him was beyond me.

'You are both still coming to John's funeral, aren't you?'

We both turned to face him; concern was etched on his bruised face.

'What do you think?' I said.

'I need you there for support. I'm having to make a speech. Please come. Don't let me down,' Charles pleaded.

He was the most self-confident person you could ever meet and could bullshit for England but he hated public speaking. The dyslexia made him get his words wrong. He knew it was garbled rubbish, but he carried on even if it didn't make sense. That sort of public humiliation tugged at your heart strings.

Monty and I exchanged a nervous look but Charles didn't notice. It was our secret now. Maybe I just had to wait?

Monty and I wrapped an arm round each other.

'We won't let you down.'

How could we?

The waitress in the short skirt skipped over. It appeared our taxis had arrived. Charles turned and kissed me on the cheek.

'Hey, I was only kidding about your wife.'

'I know,' I replied, but I wasn't sure I wanted to know the truth.

We stood outside the bar.

I hated goodbyes and as the first taxi drew up I wasn't

sure whether this was a beautiful beginning or a poignant finale. We took it in turns to hug each other and one by one we went our separate ways again. We had made our peace and shared our memories and I think in our own way we all took something life-affirming from the evening.

It was enough. I hoped we would continue our friendship, but it would be different now, the fountain of youth had been lost forever.

I realised we could never go back.

## LATER

I sat in the back of a saloon car. A Fan Orange air freshener and worry beads dangled from the rear view mirror.

The driver was Asian and wanted to talk about United's recent run of losses. It started to rain, the wipers swishing faster and faster as we headed up the hill, along the Edge and past the Wizard Restaurant. I leant back on the head rest and placed my hands over my eyes.

I removed myself to a time before I had loved and lost anything, a time before marriage and children, before the devastation of failure. A time when I hadn't prized anything greatly enough to fear the loss of it. I fought back tears. Tears that mourned what we had lost. Tears for John and his family. Tears for all of us.

I caught the driver's eye in the mirror. 'Are you alright mate? Bad news?'

I gathered myself. 'Someone died.'

'Oh. Sorry.'

'I'm fine, I just...'

Then I remembered us sitting on the bus travelling to the fancy dress party. A whole lifetime in front of us.

Mad Max, the Caveman and Greystoke.

I started to laugh, really laugh and the driver joined in even though he had no idea what I was laughing at. I wanted to tell him about us, about all the crazy times we had together, but I didn't think he would understand. It was a different universe.

In that brief moment I underwent some kind of transformation. I rubbed my eyes, wiping the tears of laughter away. Instead of remorse and regret, I felt invigorated and inspired. I knew instinctively the subject matter of my book. A true story about three friends brought back together by tragedy: a story about belonging, loyalty and the fragility of friendship.

*Until next time.*

Printed in Great Britain
by Amazon